Raven After Dark

Raven After Dark

Donald MacKenzie

HOUGHTON MIFFLIN COMPANY BOSTON

1979

For Patrick O'Callaghan

Library of Congress Cataloging in Publication Data

MacKenzie, Donald, date
  Raven after dark.
  I. Title.
PZ4.M1562Rap1979   [PR9199.3.M325]   813'.5'4 79-
13932   ISBN 0-395-28209-8

Printed in the United States of America
S 10 9 8 7 6 5 4 3 2 1

Raven After Dark

1. The Hook

THE BACK OF HIS SHIRT had been sticking to the driver's seat all the way over from Chelsea. It was Sunday afternoon with the temperature outside up in the eighties. The lobby of the Soos' riverside apartment building was cool after the heat of the street. He took the express elevator. Jerry and Louise had moved into a larger flat since their marriage, a penthouse that had been the gift of Louise's parents. There were only four apartments on the fourteenth floor. The wide, spacious corridor was well lit by end windows decorated with displays of flowers. Through these windows, high-rise buildings lifted above low haze on the north side of the Thames.

Raven leaned his thumb on the bell-push, glancing across at his reflection in the wall mirror. He had been out on deck, spraying the roses, when Jerry called. His jeans and shirt were dirty, his shoes scuffed and old. Not only that, his hair needed washing. He might have done something about his appearance, if given the time, but his friend had sounded urgent.

The Hong Kong-born cop opened the door. Soo was wearing his usual weekend uniform of Yellow Peril T-shirt, drainpipe trousers, and the ultrasoft leather boots handmade for him in Macao. He gave Raven a firm handshake.

"You must have jumped every damn light between Chelsea and here!"

They were standing in a white-painted hallway hung with flowers embroidered on silk. It was impossible to see through the opaque glass door that led through into the living room. Raven looked from it to his friend.

"What's the trouble? What's all this about?"

Soo rarely used two words when one would do if the subject matter was important. All he had asked Raven was to come as soon as he could.

"Louise'll tell you," said Soo. He opened the door into a long sunny room with two French windows to a balcony overlooking the river.

It was a room Raven was at home in. The carpet and paintings were Chinese, the furniture reproduction eighteenth-century English. Taiwan ivory blended with Georgian silver. Chairman Meow, the Abyssinian cat, was asleep on top of the cabinet that housed Soo's stamp collection. Louise Soo lifted herself on her toes. Her flat-chested body was in yellow silk and she wore her black hair in a shoulder-length pageboy cut. She kissed Raven on both cheeks and turned to make the introduction, still hanging on to his hand.

"This is John Raven, Kirstie, the friend I was telling you about. Kirstie Macfarlane."

The girl sitting on the sofa was in her late twenties, with honey-colored hair and wide-spaced eyes set in a face that was too boyish to be pretty. Raven's first impression was of pictures he had seen of the young Garbo. There was the same coltish awkwardness, the same hint of sensuality. She was wearing a gingham shirt outside velvet trousers. Her brief smile left lines in her fine skin. Raven sat down next to her. Sparrows chattered on the balcony railings. The cat opened one eye and closed it again. There was a coffeepot on a side table and three dirty cups. Raven shook his head at Soo's offer of a drink. He lit a Caporal, leaned back, and waited for someone to break the silence. It was Louise Soo who spoke, standing with her back to the wall, her long sensitive cellist's fingers laced together.

"We need your help, John."

The girl stirred on the sofa beside him and Raven shrugged. "Tell me."

Jerry Soo collected the cat and carried it to the far end of the room. He sat there, kneading its neck-fur. His wife kept her eyes fixed on Raven.

"Kirstie and I are very old friends. I had a room in her flat in Paris when I was studying at the Conservatoire. We've stayed in contact."

Raven nodded again, understanding that she was telling him this was a close relationship. Soo spoke from the distance, the impact of his words heightened by his impassiveness.

"Kirstie's brother got himself into a fix. He was sentenced to five years' imprisonment at the London Sessions and hanged himself in his cell. The inquest was on Thursday and he was cremated yesterday."

Raven turned impulsively. "That's really bad. I'm sorry."

She looked at him with fatigue-smudged eyes the color of a northern lake. "Thank you, but the worst is over. All that matters is cleaning house." Accent and vowel sounds were Canadian.

It was three years since Cathy had killed herself. The thought of a Coroner's Court revived the memory. He nodded uneasily at Kirstie Macfarlane. She looked tired but her face was as controlled as her voice, as if grief had burned emotion out of her body. The sounds of a summer Sunday drifted up from below, a call from a boat on the river, the babbling of starlings up on the guttering.

Louise crossed the room and sat beside him on the sofa. He was between the two women now, cornered. He glanced at his friend but Jerry Soo continued to stroke the cat's ears, his expression bland.

"The thing is," said Louise. "Kirstie thinks that her brother was innocent."

The Canadian girl broke in impatiently. "I *know* he was innocent. You know your own brother, for God's sake! I talked to him in prison. He was framed." There was feeling in her voice now, indignation as well as impatience.

Jerry took it up. "There's nothing at all that I can do to help. At least not officially. As far as the Yard is concerned the case is closed. You know the way these things go, John. The kid's dead, right? So someone sticks his police record in the non-Active file and that is the end of that. There's nothing I *can* do," he repeated defensively.

Raven took his time lighting his next cigarette. He slipped the Dupont back in his jeans.

"What *is* there to be done?" He was looking at no one in particular, but his question was meant for Kirstie.

Louise answered. "I've known you almost four years, Kirstie twice as long. Whenever you've come to us for help, no one's asked questions. OK, I'll accept that you and Jerry have a special relationship but I'm his wife, don't forget. Have I ever asked you questions?"

Raven shook his head. Her gentleness was added reproach. "Look," he said. "I'm obviously not making myself clear. We've got to look at the facts. From what you say, Kirstie's brother was convicted of a crime and he killed himself in jail. It's terribly sad for her, especially since she thinks that he was innocent. I can understand that Jerry can't do anything to help. My question is what can anyone do to help? Exactly what are you people hoping to prove?"

"His innocence, most of all." The Canadian girl's voice was quieter than it had been but still firm. "I want my brother's name cleared and the people who framed him punished."

Raven nodded, watching the cigarette paper smoldering. Running through his mind were a hundred similar ap-

peals, most of them based entirely on wishful thinking.
"Don't get me wrong," he ventured. "But it's very hard
to accept guilt in someone you love."

"You mean you're not impressed," challenged Kirstie.
He was aware of her nervous intensity but had to say
what he thought. "I can curb my enthusiasm," he said. "At
least from what you've told me."

She rose and hurried into the bathroom. The door was
firmly closed. Soo walked bowlegged, carrying the cat.
Raven could see him in the kitchen, squatting as he poured
milk into a saucer.

Raven winced as Louise suddenly dug her nails in his
wrist. "Pig!" she said.

He stared down at the scratches on his wrist.

"Great," he said bitterly. "Here I am on a quiet Sunday
afternoon, peacefully tending my roses . . ."

"Stop it," she said, her small cat's face angry. "*Stop* it!
This girl needs help. Don't you understand that she's been
very good to me, John?"

He nodded. "You've made your point. And you want *me*
to give her help and understanding, is that it?"

"That's right," she replied. "For Jerry and me, if that's
the way it has to be."

Soo was whistling out in the kitchen, a monotonous
snatch of a Kowloon folk song that he only remembered
when under stress.

"OK," said Raven. His weary manner was a cover for his
secret enthusiasm. Thought of the girl behind the closed
bathroom door made his adrenalin surge.

She was out in a couple of minutes, the ends of her
straight hair curling on her shoulders. She took her seat
beside Raven.

"I'm sorry," she said, almost but not quite smiling. She
made no further explanation.

Her arms and hands were brown. The only jewelry she

wore was a small green-dialed watch on a striped wrist-band.

"What do you want me to do?" Raven said impulsively.

When her smile finally did come, it came quickly, reaching up as far as her eyes.

"I'm not broke," she assured him. "It won't cost you anything."

It was a dangerous sort of statement if the implications were considered. He shrugged.

"I don't think that's too important for the moment. What's important is to have some sort of plan of action."

Louise had left the room and returned wearing a long black sleeveless dress. Her shiny black hair was caught back with a jade pin.

"Well," she said briskly. "All that's settled then. You two will want to talk things over. Jerry's driving me down to Guildford. I have a concert in two hours' time. But there's no reason why you shouldn't stay here. There's plenty of food in the refrigerator and John knows where the booze is kept."

Raven turned to Kirstie. "What do you think? Whereabouts are you staying?"

She named a hotel near Sloane Square. "Well, look," he said. "Perhaps the simplest thing is to go to my place. I have a houseboat in Chelsea Reach. I'll drive you home afterward."

Kirstie kissed Louise and Jerry. "Thanks for everything."

"We'll be in touch," Raven said smiling.

Jerry and his wife were strangely alike in that moment, boot-button eyes above oblong smiles revealing nothing of what they were thinking. Raven opened the door to the corridor.

He backed the Citroën into the alleyway next to the Herborium. The store blinds were half-drawn. Geckos dozed among bars of country soap. The interior of the place was dark and mysterious.

She barely turned her head as they passed. She had spoken little since getting into the car, answering his questions in the shortest way.

He took her by the elbow and ran her across to the other side of the Embankment. There was a faint smell of tidal water and mud, and sunshine sparkled on the river. They looked over the parapet.

"That's mine," he said, pointing down at the converted brewer's barge. The *Albatross* rose and fell lazily, squeezing the truck tires that served as buffers. The houseboat was the last in a motley string of craft, all of them permanently moored and used as homes. His neighbor's boat was a onetime river steamer that was overballasted on one side, giving it a lopsided appearance. The superstructure was painted in red and white candy stripes. A shaky network of ropes and planks connected the ten other boats to dry land.

He led the way down the steps that were cut in the granite retaining wall and unlocked the door at the end of the gangway. Her heels clattered over the metal runners. The deck was releasing the stored heat of the day, bringing out the scent of the flowers. They grew wherever there was space, in any receptacle that would hold dirt, stocks and sweet Williams in a horse trough, roses in an old bassinet.

"I like growing things," he said, as though she had asked him to justify himself.

She nodded understanding. "I wish I had the chance in Paris."

He opened the door to the sitting room. It was twenty-five by twelve feet with large windows on both sides. He pressed the button, activating the motor that pulled the curtains back. Light flooded into the room, bringing out the blues and blacks of his precious Klee. It was a comfortable room with what someone had once called "shabby elegance." The much-darned and faded Aubusson was walked on, not just hung on a wall and looked at. The big table and matching chairs had come from his parents' dining room. The rest of the house, the bedrooms and bathroom, had been refurbished two years before. But the sitting room had stayed as it was.

He chose a record at random, a Brandenburg Concerto, placed it on the turntable, and lowered the volume. Glasses and ice meant a visit to the kitchen. When he came through with the tray, Kirstie was sitting on the sofa with her back to the portside windows. She was studying the Klee, her hand over her mouth. Freak pigmentation blotched the end of her nose with an outsize freckle. He had read somewhere that a woman can look at a man and know straight away whether or not she could go to bed with him. The area of thought excited him.

"How about a drink?" he suggested.

She shifted her gaze away from the painting. "Do you have any vodka?"

He showed her the bottle from the fridge. "Wyborowa. Polish. How do you drink it?"

She frowned slightly as if trying to remember. "Straight."

He handed her the tubular glass and poured himself Scotch-and-water. When he turned, her glass was empty. He refilled it and sat down beside her.

"Cigarette?" He lifted the lid of the box. She shook her head. "OK," he said. "Let's start at the beginning."

She was holding the chilled glass against her cheek as though it gave her comfort. "I'm thirty years old," she said. "Jamie was eight years younger. My parents were divorced when I was twelve and we stayed with my father in Toronto. He never remarried."

She put her glass down and he refilled it. Maybe this was how they drank in Canada.

"My brother and I were very close until about four years ago. I'm a free-lance photographer and I had to move to Paris. As soon as I left Canada, Jamie dropped out of school. My father died the same year and Jamie had his share of what money there was. It was enough to buy the bookshop he had always said he wanted. Instead of that he took off on the Hippie Trail. I'd get cards from places like Katmandu, Delhi, and Teheran, finally Amsterdam. He called me a few times from there and then suddenly nothing. No calls, no cards. I didn't know where he was or what he was doing. Not until ten weeks ago. May I have another drink, please?"

He tilted the vodka bottle. The fingers holding her glass were as steady as her eyes.

"Don't worry," she assured him. "I can handle it."

Raven put his back against the edge of the bookcase. The movement of the boat eased the itch in his shoulder blade. Her smile switched on and off. "Jamie sent me a letter from Brixton Prison, saying that he had been arrested for stealing a painting worth a hundred and twelve thousand pounds. He needed a lawyer. It wasn't easy. The only people I knew in London were Jerry and Louise. They were the last people I wanted to go to at that time. Canada House gave me the name of a lawyer. A Mr. Lassiter. So I went to see him." She paused for a moment.

He gave her the time to continue, but she seemed to have forgotten that he was there.

"So you went to see your brother in prison," he said gently.

She nodded, holding her empty glass tightly. "That was the worst part. Jamie hated confinement even as a little boy. Seeing him there, caged like an animal, tortured me.

The years seemed to drop away and there he was, my kid brother. I would have forgiven him anything and he knew it. But there was nothing *to* forgive. He was innocent. Look, it's impossible to lie to someone you love, someone you've known all your life, right?"

He gave himself a cigarette and a refill. The sun had vanished behind the power station and the sea gulls were making tentative swoops.

"Difficult, maybe," he said. "But by no means impossible."

She shook her head at him. "We're talking about different kinds of people. Jamie *couldn't* have lied to me— therefore he was framed. He and I were the only ones who knew it. The police, the judge, the jury, none of them believed him. Can you understand how he must have felt, twenty-two years old and facing five years' imprisonment?"

He shrugged, unwilling to tell her what he really thought. That it is comparatively easy for a man in a cell to convince himself of his innocence. The sense of outrage and martyrdom will help him to survive. Only the troubled in spirit take what is called the "easy way out."

"It wouldn't have been too bad if he could have held on. He could have appealed, for instance," Raven said.

Her eyes were thoughtful. "Louise said that you used to be a cop. You talk like one. But she also said that you cared about the underdog."

"That's right," he said quietly.

She shook her head again. "You don't even know what I'm talking about, do you?"

"Wrong," he corrected. "Maybe I know too much."

The record had stopped. He flipped to the other side. She had taken a cigarette from the box and was staring at its unlit end, her hair falling over her eyes. He struck a match, suddenly feeling guilty.

"Listen to me, Kirstie. You want your brother's name

cleared, right? That's a sizable order, given the circumstances. Feelings aren't going to play any part in it. The only things that will matter are facts."

She lifted her face. "Yes." Her mouth was wide, her lips needing no embellishment. He had a sudden desire to kiss her and he wondered how she would react. Violently, probably, as though to a prize shit who was taking advantage of a girl in distress. And yet it wasn't like that. The truth was more complex. He sensed what she had to offer and he was hungry for it.

"Do you have the lawyer's address?" he asked.

She gave him a card from her purse. The name meant nothing to him. The address was in South Kensington.

"I'll keep this," he said, and put the card on his desk. "You don't happen to know the name of the officer in charge of your brother's case?"

Her hair swung as she moved her head. "I never actually went to the court. I was having to fly between here and Paris and do my work. But Jerry knows who he is."

He turned. "You look tired."

She half-smiled, half-yawned. "It's been a long day. May I use your bathroom?"

He showed her through and switched on the lights. Mrs. Burrows had put flowers in both bedrooms and the silver had a soft luster. He called a minicab service. She came back into the sitting room, touching the back of her head self-consciously.

"You've been very kind, John."

"I have my reasons," he said lightly. "A cab's on its way."

She hesitated. "When do you think you might have news for me?"

He shrugged, grinning. "Tomorrow evening. So we'd better have dinner together. I'll pick you up at your hotel at eight."

Her laugh was frank and unstrained. "OK. I'll say this

for you, John Raven. You're unlike any Englishman I've met or even heard about."

"I get better as time goes by," he promised. "Here's your cab."

He saw her to the top of the steps and waited until the hack pulled away. She did not look back. The light was starting to fade. The fishbowl lamps were on along the Embankment, yellow in the gloaming. The pair of long johns that Saul Belasus flew as a pennant hung limply from the pole. There was no sign of life on his neighbor's boat. Raven locked and bolted the gangway door as much from habit as necessity. True, there had been aggravation when he first left the police force. The circumstances behind his retirement, the drama of the Zaleski affair, had been made to order for the media. Reporters had probed Raven's life-style and background, writing pieces headed

OLD HARROVIAN THIEFTAKER CALLS IT A DAY
SCOTLAND YARD ACE BECOMES RIVER RECLUSE
SOCIETY COP MOURNS DEAD MISTRESS

He had agreed to appear once on television and refused all further interviews. But reporters continued to take pictures of him and the boat from shore, bridge, and river. His address was publicized, and disgruntled customers from the past, on temporary leave of absence from jail, tried to give him a hard time. One holed the deck of the houseboat with a lump of concrete. It all stopped the night he had borrowed Herbie. Saul Belasus' Great Dane had chased a nonswimming stringer for *Der Stern* into fourteen feet of water.

Raven sat for a while on deck, thinking about Kirstie Macfarlane the girl, rather than her problem. She had affected him more than any other woman in a long while. He found her blend of toughness and vulnerability fascinating. Suddenly it was after nine and he was hungry. Mrs.

Burrows had given up cooking and freezing meals for him, indignant at what she felt to be his ingratitude. This had been instanced by the Great Dane's retrieving a bag of *spaghetti à la carbonara* that had been destined for the sea gulls. He opened a can of corned beef, uncapped a Budweiser, and ate at the kitchen table, sitting in the half-light. It was after eleven when he picked up the phone. The Soos were home and Jerry sounded apologetic.

"I'm sorry about all that, John. It was Louise's idea. She and Kirstie are still very close and she has this loyalty thing. Do what you can, though quite frankly I don't see that there's much that *can* be done."

"She deserves a try," said Raven. "Do you know who was in charge of her brother's case?"

"George Denton. He's a D.I. on the Flying Squad."

"My God!" said Raven. "The one they call Saint George of Piccadilly?"

"None other," Soo said crisply. "The fearless foe of the underworld, the man with his mind set on higher things. Like a Commander's job, for instance."

"Do you think I could get in to see him?"

"Without a doubt. All you need is the right sort of grovel and genuflections. He's not called 'No hanky-panky Denton' for nothing. I'd sooner you didn't mention my name."

"I wouldn't think of it," said Raven. "I have to cling to what shreds of self-respect are left. Kiss Louise for me and you'll be hearing."

Morning came. It was one of those special summers, a succession of halcyon days when farmers complained, racehorse trainers complained, and the rest of the country walked, shirtsleeved, soaking up sunshine. Raven drew the curtains in his bedroom, flooding the cedarwood closets and gold carpet with light. He checked the battered traveling clock by the bedside. He had been waking at seven o'clock for the last thirty years, give or take ten minutes. His rowing machine was down in the hold, replaced by his daily jogging. He brushed his teeth, donned singlet and running shorts, and drank a glass of orange juice. Five minutes later he was trotting through the trees at the north end of Battersea Park. He no longer paid attention to the ribaldries of passers-by and was fitter than he had been in years. He was back on the boat by eight, collecting his mail and newspapers from the box at the end of the gangway. He showered and weighed himself. He'd lost three ounces since yesterday. He carried his breakfast tray back to bed.

The *Albatross* wallowed gently, sucking and grunting like a farrowing sow. His four-minute egg was perfect, the tea strong, and the toast crisp and brown. He belched, put the tray on the floor, and lit a cigarette. There was nobody around to express disapproval. The sway of the houseboat caused the doors of the clothes closet to slide in both directions. He lifted the telephone directory. Lassiter's home address was listed beneath that of his office. A woman's voice answered Raven's call. Her husband was in the bath; could he call Raven back?

Raven used the time to shave. He was fully dressed when the telephone rang.

"Mr. Lassiter? Thanks for calling back. You don't know me but I'm acting for Jamie Macfarlane's sister. I wondered if you could manage to see me sometime today?"

"You say you're acting for her. You mean you're a solicitor?"

"Just a friend," said Raven. "I'd appreciate it if you could find the time; a few minutes would do."

There was a brief pause before Lassiter answered. "It would have to be early. I'm in Bow Street at ten o'clock. Could you make it at nine? My office is on Bute Street, South Kensington."

"Nine o'clock," Raven said promptly. "I'll be there."

He left Mrs. Burrows' money with a request that she buy candles at the Scandart shop on King's Road. "The round fat ones," he wrote, his mind on his dinner date. He crossed the deck, getting a token bark from the Great Dane, who was dozing on the neighboring boat. Fifteen minutes later Raven maneuvered the Citroën into an empty parking slot on Bute Street. It was a good omen and he liked his days to start well.

Lassiter's law office was on the second story, over a betting shop. The clatter of a typewriter greeted him as he pushed the door open. A sign on a desk said RECEPTION. The girl behind it looked up.

"May I help you?"

"John Raven," he said. "To see Mr. Lassiter."

She spoke briefly into an intercom, rose, and led Raven down a corridor to a room overlooking the street. It was an untidy room, books and papers distributed without apparent sense of order. There was a dusty vase filled with dried flowers, a carpet too grimy to reveal its original color, and prints of Victorian judges. The man who welcomed Raven was soberly dressed in well-cut clothes. His hair was ginger rather than red, and his pale eyelashes gave him a slightly myopic appearance. A clock in a glass bell stood on his desk, its mechanism naked.

Lassiter waited until the girl had left the room, waved invitation at a chair, and sat down himself.

"Now," he said pleasantly. "What exactly is it that you want from me?"

Said in another way, the words could have sounded aggressive. This way they were no more than a desire for information.

Raven lit a Caporal. "As I told you on the phone, I'm trying to help Kirstie Macfarlane."

"That much I gathered," said Lassiter. "I'm still not clear what it is that you want from me."

Raven was suddenly doubtful. There were lawyers, a
high percentage of them, whose interest in a client ex-
tended no further than his acquittal or conviction. It was
an attitude that Raven could understand.

"Kirstie wants to clear her brother's name," said Raven.

Lassiter shook his ginger head. "That's a very tall order.
The only way it could be done would be through a Public
Inquiry, and you don't get those without coming up with a
lot more than we have at the moment." At least he'd
said "we."

"She's convinced that he's innocent," said Raven.

Lassiter's pale eyes closed briefly. "Look," he said when
he opened them. "I liked the kid. I was sorry for him. But
he was his own worst enemy. He'd be alive today if he
hadn't insisted on going into the witness box and giving
evidence. He didn't only lie. *He was shown to have lied.*
There's not really a great deal more to say about it."

The clock mechanism revolved soundlessly. Raven took
his eyes off it.

"You mean *you* don't think he was innocent?"

Lassiter gave himself time to consider. "It's a difficult
one to answer. OK, apart from the question of professional
etiquette. Jamie's dead and you're trying to help Kirstie.
Let's put it this way. Jamie never told the complete truth,
not even to me. I'm sure of that. But then the prosecution's
version of the affair was by no means the whole truth
either."

"Is it possible that he was framed?" demanded Raven.
"One way or another?"

"It's possible," Lassiter agreed. "And if you want to play
hunches it's even probable. But the point is that there's no
way of proving it. The boy's dead and the case is closed."

Raven kept after him. "Kirstie's alive and her brother's
name matters to her. You must have a reason for saying
what you said. I mean about a frame-up being probable."

Lassiter leaned across the desk, making a tent of his hands and elbows.

"Listen to me carefully, Mr. Raven. I'm accepting you at face value. You want to help Kirstie, fine. But there are areas into which I am not prepared to venture. I'm talking out loud, not giving a professional opinion. I wish you luck with your endeavors but I'm by no means hopeful of your success. You want to know why I said that a frame-up was possible—OK, probable. Because a lot of questions were posed at that trial that were never answered. A couple of men who, according to police evidence, played major roles in the crime were allowed to walk away from the scene. My own belief is that one of them was a police-informer. We tried to make an issue of this at the trial and got nowhere. What you have to understand, Mr. Raven, is that informers only exist for their control. For the rest of us they are faceless and nameless."

Raven knew it only too well. Seventy-five percent of criminals in the Metropolitan Police district were arrested by virtue of "information received." The sources of information were always confidential. The saying went that a copper was as good as his nark. A directive from the Commissioner of Police himself instructed his officers to protect the anonymity of their informers. They did this jealously, cosseting and grooming their protégés like managers of rival opera stars. Police behavior in this respect was both accepted and condoned by the judiciary.

"I see," Raven said slowly. "And was that your line of defense?"

Lassiter checked his watch with the clock. "I seem to be running out of time." He walked directly to a pile of tied bundles of papers and picked one out. He put it on the desk in front of Raven. "Borrow the transcript. Keep it as long as you like, so long as I get it back eventually. We had to have it done for the appeal."

"Was Macfarlane on appeal when he died?"

Lassiter nodded. "Yes, poor bastard. I'm afraid that I wasn't much use to him. What he wanted to hear was *good* news. I took the brief to one of the best men at the bar for that sort of case and he turned it down. Didn't want to touch it. I had to tell this to Jamie, that it would be a waste of time and money to go on with the appeal. He said that he'd think it over. He hanged himself the same night."

Raven gathered the bundle of typescript. "I'll see that you get this back safely. Incidentally, I'm trying to get in to see Denton."

"*Denton?*" The lawyer looked surprised. "What do you hope for there?"

Raven shrugged. "A hint—a clue. I'm not quite sure."

Lassiter shook his head slowly. "He's a merciless bastard who wouldn't wet Christ's lips on the Cross. Ruthless with a touch of insanity. Is he going to see you?"

"I haven't tried yet," said Raven.

"Then I might be able to help," said Lassiter. "He still has some of Jamie Macfarlane's personal effects that should be released to Kirstie."

He flicked the button on the intercom. "Get me Detective-Inspector Denton at Scotland Yard. The number should still be on the board."

The call came through instantly. Lassiter identified himself and winked at Raven. "I'm acting for the estate of Jamie Macfarlane. Would it be possible for someone to collect his effects? Eleven? Yes, I'm sure that would be all right. His name's John Raven. I'll give him a letter of authority." He spoke into the intercom again. "Eleven o'clock at Scotland Yard," he said to Raven. "Use the front entrance and go to the reception desk."

Raven got up. There was an irony in the situation but

he wasn't yet ready to tell Lassiter that he had been a cop himself. "I'll let you know what happens," he promised.

The girl brought in a letter, which Lassiter signed and gave to Raven. "Nice to have met you, Mr. Raven. Good luck and give my regards to Miss Macfarlane."

There was time for coffee at the Greek's café behind Scotland Yard. Raven and Jerry Soo had always used the place in preference to the police canteen. The proprietor was an old friend and sometime confidant. Raven drove the Citroën up on the sidewalk and left it nuzzling the garbage cans. The Greek owned the frontage and the car was safe from traffic wardens. The café was located on a corner with its entrance in the angle. Its position offered a two-way view from inside. Raven pushed the door open. The café was empty, the recently washed floor still drying. The walls were decorated with a bad mural of the Acropolis. The edges of a pile of paper napkins lifted in the draft from a ceiling fan. Flies were feeding from a bowl of *taramosalata*. Raven rattled his car keys on the glass counter. A man appeared in the kitchen doorway, his face and hair wet with sweat. Checked cotton trousers clung to his sturdy legs and he was wearing a T-shirt with a rag around his throat. His bare arms and shoulders were covered with springy black hair.

"Long time!" he exclaimed, coming forward and lifting the flap in the counter.

Raven winced. The Greek's embrace was a bonecrusher, his breath the essence of garlic. The Greek released Raven reluctantly, stepping back and shaking his head. "Why you don't come here no more to see me, John?"

Raven fished a bottle of Coke from the cooler. "You know the way it goes, Pantelis."

The Greek wiped the top of a table with his neck-rag and sat down facing Raven.

"Jerry still comes in allatime. So what you doing now, the life of a gentleman, I hear!"

Raven put the Coke bottle down. "A little of everything. What I really came for was your advice."

Pantelis spread his legs and his elbows, his large head cocked attentively. "Tell me!" he invited.

"It's about food," explained Raven. "I have a lady coming for dinner tonight on the boat. I don't know what to give her to eat. It would have to be something cold."

The Greek half-closed his eyes, his voice dreamy. "So where is she coming from, the lady. She English?"

"She's a Canadian living in Paris."

Pantelis swatted a fly from his neck. "She like Greek food?"

"I've no idea," said Raven.

Pantelis leered suggestively. "Firsta time, eh?" He played a few notes on an imaginary fiddle. "The lights, the wine, the music. But first the food! So you want to leave it to Pantelis, yes?"

Raven shrugged uncertainly. "It has to be something special, you understand."

The Greek looked offended. "What you think I got in my deep-freeze?" he exclaimed dramatically, pointing at the kitchen doorway. "You think I got shit in there? Why you think Goulandris eat in my brother's restaurant in Andros?"

Raven lifted a placating hand. "I know all that. You taught your brother all he knows about cooking. OK, OK. All I'm saying is that this is a special occasion. Don't worry about the cost."

The Greek's forgiving smile was enormous. "What I prepare for you," he promised, "ain't no woman in the world can resist." Someone was rattling the door handle. "*Push,* stupid," he bawled. A boy delivering milk carried in a crate of bottles.

"When could I have it?" asked Raven.

The Greek composed on his fingertips. "Come by around four o'clock."

Raven touched the Greek on the shoulder. "Thanks. I'm leaving my car outside for half an hour. I have to pay a visit to the factory."

He walked the two blocks south to New Scotland Yard, carrying the transcript of Macfarlane's trial. It was months since he had visited the concrete-and-glass complex. The main hall was thronged with plainclothesmen. Raven gave his name to a uniformed girl at the reception desk. She used a phone and offered him a token smile.

"Detective-Inspector Denton will be down in a few minutes, sir. If you'd like to take a seat over there?" She pointed at some rows of benches where people were waiting.

Raven found a place on his own. It was more than five years since he had cleared his desk up on the sixth floor and left, vowing never again to put foot in the building. Yet Fate had brought him back on several occasions. He wondered if his name still meant anything to the officers who came and went, past the security guards and into the elevators that led to the various departments. Sometimes he wondered how he had stuck it out for seventeen years. But it had never been the job that irked him, only some of the people. There'd been enough of them at the end to sour and spoil a way of life that otherwise he had enjoyed.

He turned his head, instinct telling him that the man walking across from the reception desk was Denton. Raven put the transcript behind his buttocks, neither fully out of sight nor in view.

Denton was in his late forties, slightly round-shouldered and hooknosed, with small deep-set eyes the color of slate. His blue hopsack suit and brown suede brogans had the theatrical elegance of senior Flying Squad officers. He was carrying a large manila envelope, which he placed on the bench between them.

"Mr. Raven, I presume. Do you have any identification with you?"

Raven produced Lassiter's letter, together with his driving license. The detective handed back the driving license, retaining the letter. His expression changed slightly as he caught sight of the transcript on the seat behind Raven. He emptied the large manila envelope, pushing the items along the polished wood as he enumerated them.

"One yellow metal wrist watch, marked Longines. One metal lighter. One telephone-and-address book. Various letters and papers and three hundred Dutch guilders. Macfarlane's passport was returned to the Canadian authorities after the inquest. Sign here, please." He gave Raven an official Metropolitan Police Force receipt.

Raven affixed his signature. "Did you go to the inquest yourself?"

Denton pocketed the receipt. "Of course."

"What was the verdict?"

Denton cocked his head. "You mean you don't know?"

"That's right." Raven lit a Caporal. "I know very little. I'm a friend of a friend, you might say."

"Temporary insanity," Denton replied. "They try to be kind but it all adds up to the same in the end."

Raven snapped a rubber band round the transcript and manila envelope. "There's one thing that puzzles me, Detective-Inspector. The question of insurance."

Denton's slate-colored eyes were wary. "How do you mean, insurance?"

Raven blew a stream of smoke before answering. "Well, a painting worth a hundred and twelve thousand pounds is bound to have been insured."

"Are you asking me or telling me?" Denton said dangerously.

Raven grinned and threw out his hand. "I'm asking, Detective-Inspector."

Denton was giving nothing away. "It's customary, yes."

"So a reward must have been offered for its return?"

Denton's face narrowed visibly. "I've no doubt that there was."

Raven's expression was bland. "Any idea who collected the reward? I mean the elements are all there, aren't they? Return of the stolen property, the arrest of the culprit. Whoever laid the information must have claimed the reward."

Denton buttoned his jacket deliberately. "Who told you that someone laid the information? Lassiter?"

Raven shook his head. "Nobody told me anything. I'm using common sense. Other people must have asked the same questions."

Denton's face took on the bogus innocence of a fox caught on its way out of a hen-run. "What exactly is your interest in all this, Mr. Raven? I mean, what are you trying to prove?"

"Kirstie Macfarlane still thinks that her brother was innocent."

"I see," said Denton. "Well, let me tell you something that you don't appear to appreciate. It isn't the police who determine people's guilt and put them inside. It's the judge and the jury."

"No such thing as a wrongful conviction?" asked Raven.

"There's the odd one that slips through the net," allowed Denton. "But you can be sure of this. If you're in possession of any real evidence of Macfarlane's innocence, the police would be the first to help."

Raven nodded. "I happen to know a little about police work myself."

Denton climbed to his feet, dominating Raven, who was still on the bench. "I'll accept that you have Miss

Macfarlane's interests at heart. But watch your step! The world doesn't see her brother in quite the same way as she does. The record shows that he was convicted of a serious crime and sentenced to five years for it. And the record shows that he's dead. Remember those two things and you're less likely to make a fool of yourself."

Raven carried the sound of Denton's voice with him out into the bright sunshine. The cop's last speech had been delivered with a mixture of patronage and discouragement, a kind of timely admonition to a layman who obviously didn't know the real score. Nevertheless, the question of insurance was plainly a sensitive area.

2. John Raven

IT WAS half-past eleven. Raven bought himself a turkey-on-rye and a can of beer and took them into St. James's Park. He was ahead of the office workers who flooded into the parks with their lunch later on. The only people he had to avoid were the American and Australian matrons in their butcher-blue pants, with their loaded cameras. He found a quiet spot under a lime tree near the lake. Spray fell on the grass from a nearby fountain but there was enough room to prop a deck chair against the tree trunk and stay dry. He finished his sandwich and beer, took off his shirt, and emptied the contents of the envelope onto his lap. There was no way of telling whether or not this was all Macfarlane had been carrying at the time of his arrest. The address book was an old one, with half the entries crossed out or amended. He found Kirstie Macfarlane's Paris address and telephone number. Names and places ranged from Toronto to Kabul but there was no link with anyone living in England. Macfarlane's watch was a medium-priced model with an automatic movement, the lighter a throwaway. There was nothing that gave a clue to the dead man's personality. Raven put the articles back in the envelope and opened the transcript.

Sixty-four pages of bond paper typed with an electric typewriter gave the document an appearance of authenticity. REGINA v. MACFARLANE, like the main bout on

some fight bill. He started to read the transcript of the
court reporter's notes, leaning back, the smell of the lime
tree sweet in his nostrils. Ducks paddled in the water a few
feet away. He finished the transcript without stopping and
then started to reread. It was important to detach a thread
of narrative from the bald series of questions and answers.
It was more than an hour before the picture emerged with
any clarity. Macfarlane's story went like this.

A Peter van Eyck self-portrait valued at £112,000 had
been stolen from the Gloucestershire home of a lady called
Kennett early in 1978. The police had been informed but
their inquiries had met with no success. A year later, officers stopped a hired car driven by Jamie Macfarlane and
the stolen painting had been found in the trunk. These
facts were undisputed by prosecution and defense alike;
the rest of the action was bitterly disputed by both sides.

Briefly stated, the prosecution's case was that, as a result
of having received certain information, Detective-Inspector Denton and other police officers had been keeping
observation on a Bayswater hotel. They saw a cab
arrive with two passengers. The cab stopped near the hotel
and one of the two men went inside. Shortly afterward he
emerged with Jamie Macfarlane. The second man now left
the cab carrying an oblong parcel wrapped in brown
paper. This parcel was placed in the trunk of Macfarlane's
hired car. The lid of the trunk was left open. Denton
testified that all three men appeared to be looking down
into the trunk while Macfarlane consulted a magazine he
was holding in one hand. The trunk was closed on the
wrapped parcel and one of the men drove off in the taxi.
Macfarlane and the second man went back into the hotel.
Shortly afterward they reappeared and drove away in
Macfarlane's hired car. Detective-Inspector Denton followed in an unmarked police vehicle together with other
officers in more cars. The police officers kept in touch by

radiophone. Macfarlane drove to an address in South London, staying in the car while his passenger went into a block of flats. A quarter-hour passed and the passenger had not returned. Macfarlane now left the car and appeared to be looking for the other man. Finally he returned to the car and drove off at high speed. He was stopped in Fulham by Detective-Inspector Denton and other officers and taken to Chelsea Police Station, where he was searched. A copy of *Art and Antiques* was found in his overcoat pocket, open at a page that displayed a colored photograph of the van Eyck self-portrait. Underneath the photograph was the legend "STOLEN—£11,200 reward subject to the usual conditions. Lee, Ungar and Hilary, Insurance Assessors, 29 St. Michael's Street W.2."

The brown paper parcel was taken from Macfarlane's car and opened in his presence. It was found to contain the stolen painting. Macfarlane was asked to explain how it came to be in his possession. His reply was that he had not known that the painting inside the wrappings was a van Eyck nor that it had been stolen. He was subsequently charged with the theft and committed from West London Magistrates Court for trial at Knightsbridge Crown Court.

The main weight of the cross-examination fell on Denton. He was asked whether the nature of his information had given him cause to believe that a crime would be committed. His answer was affirmative. This was why he had had the hotel under observation. Since he had seen what he must have known to be the stolen painting delivered, he was asked why he allowed the two men who had brought it and the cabdriver to escape. His excuse was that this had been a matter of expediency. The nature of the stake-out, his own position on the street, had made communication with other officers difficult at that particular moment. He had judged it better to let the first man go in the taxi rather than lose Macfarlane, the painting, and the second man.

The second man's disappearance later he explained by saying that he had not known that the block of flats had a rear exit. Challenged, he denied that he had seen Macfarlane talking to anyone outside the apartment block and that he definitely had not planted the copy of *Art and Antiques* on the Canadian.

Raven took a rest for a while, looking for the holes in Denton's evidence. The obvious ones had been plugged for him by the judge, who instructed the jury that informers were a fact of life, no matter how repugnant the idea might be. Police officers had the right if not the duty to protect their sources of information.

Raven started rereading Macfarlane's version. It was too lightweight surely to be an outright invention. Any street-corner scalawag with a sense of self-preservation could have concocted a more likely story. He testified that he had come to England from Amsterdam where he had been for almost a year, earning his living by dealing in antiques that he bought for the most part in England. This was a buying trip and he was carrying three thousand dollars, Canadian. He'd picked up a rented car at the airport and driven to a hotel in Bayswater. He was up early the following morning, before seven o'clock, the hour when business started in the Bermondsey Antique Market. Shortly after arriving he was accosted by a man he knew as Joe, a casual acquaintance, who was a market runner, half-tout half-hustler, a man who took a small percentage on deals he was involved with. Joe told Macfarlane that he knew someone with a good painting for sale. The man was short of cash and a profitable deal could be arranged. He offered to bring the painting to Macfarlane's hotel for inspection and Macfarlane agreed. He had bought paintings before and sold them in Holland at a profit. Joe arrived at the hotel later that morning saying that the painting was with a second man outside in a taxi. The man who owned it would be joining them shortly. At this moment the phone rang, a call for Joe. The owner had changed his mind and wanted them to go to an address in South London where the deal could be discussed.

At this point the brown-paper-wrapped parcel was brought from the taxi and placed in the trunk of Macfarlane's car. The second man drove off in the cab while Macfarlane drove Joe to the address in South London. Joe went into a block of flats, saying that he was going to fetch the owner of the painting. There was no sign of him after twenty minutes and Macfarlane began to get nervous. He got out of the car and started to look for Joe near the entrance to the block of flats. There was no sign of Joe but someone else appeared, someone who beckoned Macfarlane into the shelter of the entrance. Something had come up. Macfarlane was to leave immediately and take the painting with him. They'd be in touch with him later. Then this man vanished in turn. By now, said Macfarlane, he was suspicious as well as nervous and badly wanted to get rid of the parcel in his car. But it wasn't his and he was scared, knowing that violence was a part of the shady world of street markets. He thought of going to the police but decided against it, at least for the moment. He remembered that a Canadian friend called Neil had a bookstore on Fulham Road. Neil had lived in London for twelve years and knew his way around. He'd be the one to advise Macfarlane the best course to take. Macfarlane had been on his way to Neil's shop when the police stopped him. He had never seen the copy of *Art and Antiques* that was supposed to have been found in his pocket. He hadn't known that the painting in his car was a Peter van Eyck or that it was stolen.

The prosecution counsel's cross-examination made a

fool of him. Asked why he hadn't made inquiries about the
painting when it was first offered to him, the name of the
artist, the style or period, Macfarlane replied that it simply
hadn't occurred to him. He said that he found it normal to
drive off with a man he barely knew and a painting he
hadn't seen to a totally unfamiliar address. Told that three
police officers had had him in full view at the block of flats
and had not seen him talk to anyone, Macfarlane insisted
on his story of the warning stranger.

Raven read the opening speech of the defense counsel.
He knew the court and could imagine the scene. Macfarlane in the dock, pale after six weeks of awaiting trial, the
judge and counsel in their wigs and gowns, uncomfortable
in the heat of a June afternoon. The room would have
gone silent as defense counsel rose to speak.

"Ladies and gentlemen of the jury. This is the third day
of this trial and some of you may be wondering why these
proceedings were brought in the first place. Be that as it
may, you have listened patiently to the evidence and persuasive closing speech of my learned friend. I use the word
'persuasive' advisedly because that is precisely what Mr.
Savitt is trying to do, he is trying to persuade you to reach a
verdict that is in conflict with the evidence. No matter what
opinion one forms about this case, one thing is certain. The
conduct of the police officers leaves a bad taste in the
mouth. A number of questions remain unanswered.

"My friend accuses me of making a deliberate attack on
the officers concerned and this is a serious accusation. The
police in this country have a deserved reputation for up-
rightness, for being elevated above everything that is mean
and devious. But one bad apple can spoil the barrel and we
must never forget that the police too are human. It is
sometimes very tempting to cut corners when your mind is
already made up about a certain issue. The truth is that in

this case the police genuinely believed that in dealing with Mr. Macfarlane they were dealing with a crook. I intend to show you that they were wrong, wrong in their conception of this idea and wrong in their method of pursuing it. . ."

Raven paused to reflect. These were stirring words but the jury hadn't been swayed. The record showed that they had retired to their room at three minutes past eleven and that they returned at eleven-forty, taking thirty-seven minutes to arrive at a unanimous verdict. The sentencing judge had wasted little time with exhortation.

"Jamie Macfarlane," he said. "The jury has found you guilty of dishonestly handling a painting while knowing or believing it to have been stolen. A verdict with which I agree wholeheartedly. You have been skillfully defended and I have listened carefully to everything that has been said on your behalf. It was pointed out that you have never been in trouble before but there is a first time for everyone. I have little doubt that the real reason for this is that you happened not to be caught. You are a young man from a good background who has turned his talents deliberately to crime. Well, it is the policy of this court, at least, to discourage this sort of behavior. You will go to prison for a term of five years."

Raven opened his eyes and stared out across the water. Geese were cropping grass on the island, indifferent to the tourists and their Instamatics. Without exactly knowing why, he felt that there was something wrong in what he had just read. As Lassiter said, too many questions remained unanswered. He snapped the elastic back on the transcript and started across the park in the direction of the Greek's café. Pantelis had the food waiting, packed in plastic containers. He lifted one cover after another, grinning proudly. The long Kalamata olives were purple in color and stuffed with anchovies, the Mediterranean

tomatoes coarse-skinned and misshapen but with pulp as
sweet as honey. There were stuffed vine-leaves, *homma,* and
the flat Middle East bread; Pantelis' homemade *taramosalata*—smoked cod's roe, milk-soaked bread, garlic, oil,
and lemon. The leaves had been left on the peaches and
apricots. Goat cheese completed the menu.

"You like?" beamed the Greek.

Raven nodded. It was impossible to resist Pantelis' enthusiasm and the meal looked superb. "How much is all
this?"

Pantelis held up ten fingers. "Because you are my friend.
Is a feast of love and no lady refuse, you unnerstan'?"

Raven gave the Greek the ten pounds he asked for and
added two more. It had been a brilliant idea, coming to
Pantelis. The alternative would have been Mrs. Burrows'
precooked *escalopes,* pale meat in soggy bread crumbs, or
some of his own scrambled eggs.

"Thanks a lot, Pantelis."

The Greek rummaged through the black hair at the
base of his throat. "The Chinaman was in. He know your
lady?"

"The Chinaman knows everything," Raven assured him.
"Stay out of mischief."

It was four-twenty when he parked in the alleyway by the
Herborium. Saul Belasus and the Great Dane were seated
in two cane chairs, apparently asleep. Raven sidestepped
through the traffic, carrying the food and the transcript.
Mrs. Burrows had been and gone. The candles he had
asked her to buy were on the kitchen table. He covered this
with a damask cloth that had been his mother's and set it
with the last of the Raven silver. The meal would have to be
served from the dresser. He cut some red roses and put a
bottle of Krug in the refrigerator. Then he opened all the

windows. The whole boat stank of furniture polish. He put the envelope with Macfarlane's effects in the sitting room and checked the telephone number of the insurance company. A representative of the company had testified to the value of the painting and the address had been recorded in the transcript. He dialed the number.

A girl's voice answered. "Lee, Ungar and Hilary."

"Good afternoon. I'd like to speak to someone about a reward that you advertised."

"One moment, please." He heard her busy with her switches and then a man's voice. "Claims. Kent speaking."

"It's about the reward for the return of the Peter van Eyck self-portrait."

"I see. And in what particular context?"

"The context of payment," Raven said clearly.

"May I have your name, please?"

Raven gave his address for good measure. "The announcement said that the reward would be paid on the usual conditions. I take it that means the return of the painting and the arrest of the people who stole it?"

Kent's tone was suddenly cooler. "Do you mind telling me what your interest is in this matter, Mr. Raven?"

"Not at all. A man was sentenced to five years' imprisonment for stealing that painting. I'm trying to find out if the reward has been paid."

"I see," Kent said again. Reflection didn't seem to do too much for him. "Let's get one thing clear. Are you claiming the reward yourself?"

"Absolutely not. I just told you my interest. I'm trying to determine whether or not the reward has been paid."

Another pause appeared to make Kent's mind up for him. "I'm afraid I'm not at liberty to divulge this sort of information, certainly not on the telephone. If you have any further inquiries, I suggest that you put your questions on paper and address them to one of our partners. And, by the way, this conversation has been recorded."

"I'm not surprised," said Raven. "It's getting so that you can't trust anyone."

He replaced the receiver, remembering the magazine that was supposed to have been found on Macfarlane. Since the Canadian flatly denied having seen it before, why hadn't it been tested for fingerprints?

He went out on deck and smoked another Caporal. One of the houseboats upstream was hung with wet wash that was gently steaming in the afternoon sunshine. Raven poked around in his flower containers looking for the detested greenfly. The wallflowers were a present from his sister and conjured up a faint memory of a Suffolk manorhouse and the parents he barely remembered.

He straightened his back very carefully. He had taken a bad fall from a horse in the Camargue the year before and was solicitous for his bones. He watered the plants, running the film of the day's action in his head. It was satisfactory, he decided, without being spectacular. Lassiter was a possible credit, Denton an almost certain loss. He hosed the deck, pleased that he managed to give some pigeons a soaking. He coiled the hose and went inside.

The cream-painted kitchen didn't look too bad even in this light. He put the roses on the table. The silver was bright on the bog-oak Welsh dresser. With the curtains drawn and the candles lit, the door hooked back to offer fresh air and a glimpse of the sitting-room, it would be a civilized scene. It excited him to think that in an hour or so he'd be sitting across the table from Kirstie, locked into whatever the game was that they were playing. He anointed himself with Paco Rabanne and put on a clean blue linen shirt and bleached jeans that had been boiled to softness. Mrs. Burrows had a way with water and soda. A pair of Indian sandals completed his outfit.

Looking into the full-length mirror, he found himself thinking again about Denton. Macfarlane's lawyer had been right. Cops with a sense of dedication often tended to cut corners. Ambitious ones did the same thing. It was easy to salve your conscience when you knew deep inside you that a man was guilty; it was common practice to drop the planted evidence or rig the confession. His feeling was that this was what had happened in the case of Denton and Macfarlane.

3. Smiling Jack Jubal

THE CEMETERY RAILINGS bordered the entire length of one side of the road. Opposite was a row of three hundred cheaply built houses, two-up and two-down, with grimy brickwork and yards covered with filth. The acacia trees in front were stunted and sickly. He pulled up fifty yards from the cemetery entrance, scanning the vehicles that were parked in both directions. There was no sign of Denton's car but then that was Denton's style. On a trip like this he'd use public transport, a bus probably, then sneak into the cemetery through a side entrance. It was a stupid place to fix a rendezvous but that too was part of Denton's performance. Detective-Inspector Denton, a fearless member of the Flying Squad, an arch-fucker who'd put his own cousin inside. Put strangers away if you like but not your own.

Smiling Jack locked the big silver Jaguar, trying each door carefully. This was a neighborhood where they had your trousers off if you bent to tie a shoelace. He bought a large bunch of chrysanthemums from the flower-seller at the cemetery gates. The smile he offered the man had nothing to do with his mood. It was habitual and he sometimes smiled for long periods during his sleep. He stood in the central avenue, squinting into the evening sun and seeking his bearings. He was built on the short side with too much of his weight in the upper part of his body. His hair was the color of weathered straw and hung flat about his ears. It was cut in a fringe. He was wearing a gray suit, black tie, and black alligator shoes. He was proud of his feet and did the best he could for them.

The cemetery was laid out in a gridiron pattern, its fifty acres cut in two by the central avenue, with blacktop walks leading off on each side. A forest of gravestones marked plots that were covered with grass, gravel, or weeds. Sunlight glistened on plastic shields protecting plastic flowers. Ahead of him was a woman leading a child by the hand toward the nondenominational chapel. Smiling Jack took one of the northbound pathways. It was deserted ground with the graves old, dug a hundred years before. Family tombs were an example of bygone craftsmanship, the joints in the marble and granite sealed with lead.

Denton was sitting halfway along the walk with an unwrapped handful of flowers beside him. Smiling Jack placed his bouquet next to it and sat down heavily, resting his palms on his knees. There was no one closer to them than a groundsman clipping a yew hedge a couple of hundred yards away. Smiling Jack turned his head slowly.

"What made you pick a fucking cemetery? All London to choose from and he picks a bleedin' cemetery! What do you want to see me for, anyway?"

If you ignored the hair, Denton looked like a collie in wraparound sunglasses. He leaned back, elegant in blue hopsack, an arm extended along the bench. "You're in dead trouble, mate, and it could be serious."

Smiling Jack frowned. When you looked at him closely, Denton had teeth like a dog as well, long yellow canines.

"What kind of trouble are you talking about?"

Denton shifted the gum he was chewing. "Who collected that money in the end?"

Smiling Jack stared off into the distance. "What difference does that make?"

"Answer the question," said Denton.

Smiling Jack shrugged, uncomfortable at the turn the conversation was taking.

"George Smith," he said defensively. "You told me to give you a name and I did. George Smith picked the money up and George Smith signed for it."

Denton showed his long teeth. "Then you'd better tell George Smith that someone's on his tail. Someone's been inquiring about him at the insurance company's offices. Someone with a habit of poking his nose into other people's business."

"Jesus!" said Jubal. The gardener was approaching, wheeling a load of yew clippings. Both men waited until he had passed, Jubal picking his nose reflectively.

Denton enlarged. "He came to see me this morning, this guy. Macfarlane's lawyer sent him over to collect some stuff. Then this afternoon he called the insurance people. I had them on the line asking if he had any connection with Macfarlane's case."

"Jesus," Jubal repeated. With Macfarlane putting a rope around his neck the whole business was supposed to be over and done with. Denton's news was disturbing. "Have you got any idea who this bastard is?" he inquired.

Denton nodded. "No problem there. I had his form five minutes after he left the building. He's an ex-cop himself. Someone called Raven, a D.I. from the Yard who retired a few years ago after some sort of dust-up. He's been into all kinds of stuff since then, a real shit-stirrer. He's the guy that got that Commander seven years not so long back."

Jubal was no longer listening. He had heard too much already. "Something'll have to be done. I said, something'll have to be done," he repeated more loudly.

"I heard you," Denton answered easily. "And if I were you I'd make it fast."

Jubal blinked. He had a feeling that he was being abandoned and he didn't like it. "You're right," he said. "We can't afford to have too many questions asked about that trial."

Denton's eyes were hidden behind his sunglasses but his voice was cool. "You don't have to worry about the trial. You're safe enough there. It's George Smith who has to worry."

The gulf Denton was putting between them was growing. "It was your idea to fit him up," Jubal said defensively.

"*Was* it?" Denton said casually. "All I remember is that some asshole, a notorious police-informer, told me that a crime was about to be committed. A Canadian he knew was on the point of buying a stolen painting. I took the appropriate measures."

Jubal wet his lips. "What about the letter you wrote to the insurance company?"

"*Me?*" Denton gave a little chortle. "The Commissioner of Police wrote the letter certifying that George Smith was the name of the informant."

Jubal mopped his neck with his handkerchief. "Whose side are you on anyway, Denton?"

"Mine," said Denton. "But it could be yours too. You've had almost twelve grand out of that deal—now you've got to earn it. Make sure that Raven gets discouraged."

Jubal looked doubtful. "He doesn't sound the sort who discourages easy."

"He's a gentleman," Denton said sarcastically. "Harrow School. And gentlemen don't like violence. Here's his address—a houseboat in Chelsea Reach—and his phone number."

Jubal took the piece of paper. "Typical, ain't it? No problems, you said. Twelve grand for a few days' work and now this. Raven's as much your problem as mine."

Denton shook his head. "You're wrong there. You're forgetting that I'm an officer of the law who did his duty right down the line. I collared the culprit and protected your fair name. If trouble does come I can always walk away from it."

"And you would?" challenged Jubal.

"Try me," said Denton.

Jubal stared down at his neatly shod feet. He'd been living dangerously for five years, turning in people he knew, trading information for the insurance reward. Up to now it had always gone smoothly with Denton. Each had known what the other wanted. Denton climbed fast with a series of spectacular captures and convictions. Jubal took the money.

"Relax," said Denton. "Raven doesn't know much as yet. The insurance people wouldn't answer questions. But if he does start backtracking, he just might turn something up."

Jubal thought about it for a while, under no illusions as to where he stood. Denton would drop him overboard without a qualm. Jubal rose and threw his flowers on the nearest grave,

"Leave it to me. I'll think of something."

"Leave it to you?" Denton removed his sunglasses. His eyes were cold and speculative. "I can think of people who've done a whole lot less damage than you have and finished up dead or crippled for life. You've been lucky, Smiler. Nobody knows you for the shit you really are. No one but me, that is."

In fact the thought was never very far from Jubal's mind. A chance look or remark could trigger the sudden fear that he'd been exposed. Yet he pushed himself to the limit, visiting people he had put in jail and listening to their vengeful tales of betrayal.

"I've always held up my end of the bargain," he said.

Denton put his sunglasses on again. "Yes, you have, and I admire a man who knows what's good for him. It means

that he's going to be around for a while. I'll give you a bell
tonight."

A look of concern vied with Jubal's smile and won. "Give
it a rest with the phone calls, will you?" he whined. "It
makes my old lady nervous and there's the kids."

"Then you ring me." The number Denton gave to Jubal
was a new one. "My Bible-study class," Denton said, grinning. "I'll be there until midnight. Ask for Mr. Denton and
watch your language."

He placed his flowers on the grave next to Jubal's, wiped
his hands, and disappeared.

Jubal unlocked the Jaguar. The leather upholstery
creaked as he settled himself in the driver's seat. It gave
him pleasure to own the best. A lot of mugs banged on
about the benefits of socialism but all that was shit. When
you worked it out, the government only doled out what
they took off you in the first place. And their democracy
they could shove. You had to fight for whatever you got in
this life. Nobody gave you nothing except maybe your
parents and his hadn't given him much. Not that there'd
been a lot to give. The old man had driven a horse and cart
around London, snow, rain, and sunshine, buying his bits
of lead piping and copper. He was poor, he'd said, but he
was honest. And a lot of good that had done him. Nobody
in the family had ever taken a holiday and he couldn't
remember anyone in the house kissing or saying, Happy
Christmas. One of his earliest memories was of his father
sitting in the outside lavatory with his cap on and the door
open, the horse watching him from across the stableyard.

He switched on the motor and put the gearshift in drive.
Home was a five-bedroom house facing Richmond Park,
postwar Queen Anne, and built of soft red brick. White-
painted gates protected a half-hoop of blacktop. The rose
bushes were showing splashes of vivid color. He rolled

down the ramp to the three-car garage, frowning as he saw the oil-stained concrete where his wife parked her Volkswagen. He must have told her fifty times that the right place for oil was in the bleedin' motor but Millie always seemed to cock a deaf 'un. She'd been like that ever since the twins were born five years before, never listening to what he said and giving forth with a whole lot of backchat. She had no respect for him anymore and sooner or later he was going to have to do something about it.

At the moment they weren't seeing enough of one another to make it worthwhile to start any arguments. The business took up most of her time and she'd actually started to make a profit. A bit of a feat, come to think of it, with a rent of two grand and four fag stylists to pay. No wonder she was charging seven and eight quid for a haircut and what's more she was getting it.

He walked round to the back of the garage and let himself into the house. The kitchen door was wide open and there was no sign of the dog. He could hear the twins shouting in the pool at the far end of the garden, a hundred and fifty yards away. He went to the window. The Swedish *au pair* was standing on the diving board, watching them, dressed in a bikini. Millie claimed that the girl was a slut, but in her book any eighteen-year-old with an ass like an angel's would be a slut. He had a flash of grievance at the absence of the Doberman. Bleedin' good, wasn't it— back door wide open and the dog locked up somewhere! It was an open invitation to the spade boosters who came up from Brixton and Clapham, gangs of them, ripping off anything that wasn't screwed down. Not that they'd show much profit from the half-ton safe up in the bedroom. But they weren't burglars as much as vandals, destroying things for the sake of destruction. Bastards.

He called the dog's name and heard the answering scratching. He opened the door to the downstairs lavatory.

A one-eyed Doberman charged past him, tail-stump wagging, through the kitchen door to his favorite spot under the big beech tree. The vantage point allowed the dog to control most of the house and garden.

Jubal changed into slacks, a Windbreaker, and loafers, and took a roll of twenty-pound notes from the safe. As always, he was conscious of the need to present the correct image. The house was in Millie's name and the neighbors referred to him as "that nice Mr. Jubal." The *au pair* took the twins to kindergarten and sometimes he collected them. None of the neighbors had ever asked him what he did for a living, though had they done so he would have had the answers ready.

He let himself out through the front door, walked to Richmond Station, and took a taxi from the stand outside. The driver let him off in Bermondsey. Jubal walked toward the river, crossing the cobblestones between warehouses reeking of the sweet pungency from the brewery. The neighborhood had had its day. The wharves were mossgrown, the warehouse windows boarded up or broken. It was a district that was almost deserted at night, silent then except for the occasional shout or scream that was never investigated.

He climbed three flights of uncarpeted stairs to a landing. The sign on the door read

BERMONDSEY BRIDGE CLUB   MEMBERS ONLY

He narrowed his nostrils on remembered smells, chaff cut long ago mingling with the heady aroma of barley and hops. He had grown up in a cold-water cottage a quarter-mile away. He'd been out of the neighborhood for twenty-five years but coming back always gave him a *frisson* of fear, a reminder of what he might still have been. He turned the door handle, meeting the stench of beer and tobacco and maintaining his smile. Men were playing poker and two-handed rummy, bottles on the green baize between them. A couple of them looked up briefly and returned to their cards.

Jubal went through a door at the far end of the smoke-filled room. The man sitting with his feet on the table was in his fifties and had a hairless head like a skull. His eyes and his cheeks were sunken and his clothes hung loosely on his bony frame. He pushed his hand out of his sleeve, his face as mournful as an undertaker's mute.

"Jesus, Smiler! How are you? What are you up to, mate?"

A canary in a cage hung near the window. Smiling Jack wiped the seat of a chair and sat.

"Up and down, Dasher. Up and down. How about yourself?"

It was dangerous to appear too prosperous, a loss of reputation to admit to any sort of failure. The correct formula lay somewhere in between.

Dasher took his feet from the table and popped a mint in his mouth.

"I don't get no sleep," he complained. "By the time them slags outside are gone I'm wide awake. What can I do for you?"

Jubal lit a cheroot. The clothes he was wearing came from a chain store but his loafers were handmade.

"I want a little job done, Dasher. A geezer's been stepping out of line. He's got to be taught a lesson."

Dasher looked at the ceiling. Plaster dangled from the lathes where part of it had collapsed.

"You come at a bad time, Smiler. The boys aren't that keen since the Law dug up Aussie Joe. Someone could have done a lot of bird over that one. People get discouraged. You know how it is."

"I know how it is," agreed Jubal. He wondered how the canary managed when Dasher closed the club. It looked half-starved as it was. "But this is different. I'm not trying to get someone planted. Teach him a lesson is all. An arm or a leg."

"Ah," said Dasher reflectively. "That's different. But it'll cost you," he warned sharply.

Jubal blew his nose in a tissue and inspected the result. Dasher seemed not to notice his surroundings, which was hardly surprising when you remembered that he had done fourteen years in prison, ten of them in solitary, for a murder people said he knew nothing about.

"Of *course,* it'll cost me," said Jubal. "Nobody comes to you for charity. If he did, he'd want his head examined."

Dasher sucked in his cheeks. "I don't think you're old enough to give me lip."

"I'm old enough," Jubal assured him. "And I'm sassy enough."

Dasher negotiated another mint. "I don't know that much about you but I do sometimes wonder. Mystery X, the geezer who's into everything but never actually appears on the scene. Know what I mean?" He cocked his head, smiling approvingly as the canary let out a feeble cheep.

"I know exactly what you mean," said Jubal. "You mean that I'm not one of these stupid fuckers who advertise every time they make a score. There are two kinds of people, Dasher. Those who use their heads, the others are wankers. Where'd you get the name Dasher, anyway?"

"A bird give it to me," Dasher said primly. "A long time ago."

"I'll buy that," said Jubal. "How much is this going to cost me?"

"Three hundred," said Dasher. "Two up front. There won't be nothing in it for me but then I wouldn't want to earn off you, would I?"

"Never," said Jubal. Dasher would take the lion's share and give his cowboys fifty apiece but protocol required the charade of comradeship. He peeled off ten twenty-pound notes and added a slip of paper bearing Raven's address and telephone number. "It's all there, guy by the name of John Raven. He lives on this houseboat in Chelsea Reach. Will your people stand up? I mean, are they reliable?"

Dasher half-closed his eyes. His shoulders shook with merriment.

"What's so funny?" demanded Jubal. "What are you grinning at?"

Dasher's eyes opened. "You don't come round here too often. You've lost your sense of judgment. Your sense of judgment's all fucked-up. These are not your wind-up tearaways. These are real pros. OK, young if you like but real pros."

Jubal wet his lips delicately. The room, with its torn ceiling and filthy floorboards, was suddenly oppressive. Dasher was right. He didn't belong here anymore. "It's got to be done tonight," he insisted.

"That shouldn't be any problem." Dasher indicated the dusty telephone. "I can get it in the works in a couple of minutes. Does this guy live alone?"

"I don't know *how* he lives," said Jubal. "I'm buying, not selling."

Dasher cracked the knuckles on his right hand. "You got to make things easy for people, as easy as you can. How bad do you want him hurt?"

The canary flicked a seed from its cage. Jubal brushed it from his lap.

"The fucker's out of order. I want him to understand that he's not to poke his nose in other people's business."

Dasher popped another mint and spoke with his mouth full.

"You mean you want a verbal to go with it."

Jubal shook his head. "Forget the frills. Just do as I ask. I want it done tonight, remember."

"Don't worry," Dasher said expansively. "Give me a bell later. I'm here till two in the morning. You still got that timber yard?"

Jubal wiped the seat of his trousers. "Yes."

"A good business, timber," said Dasher. "I mean wood. A clean smell."

"That's right," said Jubal. The timber yard was the nearest any villain came to his front of respectability. The trail stopped there. "I'll call you later."

Dasher nodded. "Stay lucky, mate."

Jubal closed the door behind him. How did he mean, "Stay lucky?" There'd been a couple of cracks like that, delivered in a way that suggested that Dasher knew more than he was saying. Yet what *could* he know, what could anyone know? This business was making him nervous. He needed a holiday. He made his way through the card-players. He picked up another cab near the bridge that took him back to Richmond. Self-protection had become second nature to him. He was well-versed in the art of survival by the time he had reached the age of fifteen, knowing too much for predatory homosexuals and keeping his eyes averted when on hostile territory. He learned the art of displacement, the trick of not being where he was expected to be. An alibi became a fact of life. If you heard that something was about to go off, it mattered not that you had no part in the caper, you made sure that your appearance was on record as being elsewhere at the appropriate moment.

He leaned back in the cab and lit another cheroot. There were those who wouldn't do business with Dasher. They said he was stir-crazy, that he'd spent too much time inside, and it was common knowledge that he mixed with fags and psychos. But he got things done. Jubal had used him half a dozen times over the years and the ex-con had always delivered. Nevertheless, he thought, the thing to do here was get himself home and invite a couple of Millie's free-loading friends to the house. While Dasher's cowboys were on the rampage, the Jubal hearth would strike a note of quiet domesticity. Millie'd be belting the gin and banging on about what a great head she had for business. Also present, as the gossip columns said, would be Mrs. Dave Sugarman, widow of the well-known manufacturing furrier, and Nell Harrigan, sole survivor of Liz Mandler's Downtown Frolics.

Thinking back, it was odd the way he'd become involved with the painting in the first place. It had been just after Easter. He'd been going to Bermondsey Market a couple of times a month. He liked the scene, the bustle of the street, though it was seven o'clock in the morning, the rows of stalls under the lamps, the furtive deals being done in the cafés and tea-bars. Most of all, it was a great place for gossip, a rendezvous for crooked entrepreneurs. Cautious, he never chased a lead but was always ready to listen.

It had been drizzling that morning and there were beads of moisture on "Sir" Sidney Rawling's Guardee mustache and camel's-hair overcoat. Sir Sidney was a conman who specialized in conning his own kind. A judicious use of public transport protected him from serious injury. He came to Jubal with a proposition. He, Sir Sidney, had a valuable painting for sale, a Peter van Eyck self-portrait. The painting, he related, had belonged to his ex-wife who still laid claim to it. Under the circumstances Sir Sidney would accept a bargain price of two thousand pounds, no checks and no bartering. The painting, he said, could be seen at Waterloo Station, where it was presently kept in a locker. Jubal arranged to meet Sir Sidney at two o'clock that afternoon and went straight to the Central Reference Library. An art book identified the painting as "painted on wood in oils, 18 x 12 inches." A back number of the *Metro-*

politan Police Gazette informed him that the painting had
been stolen from a Cotswold mansion six months before. A
reward of £11,200 was being offered for its return.

At two o'clock Sir Sidney had been waiting under the
clock in the concourse in Waterloo Station when he was
approached by two men who produced police warrant
cards. They searched his person and removed the key to the
locker. Sir Sidney was taken to a car and driven around for
the next hour or so. He was later released twenty-eight
miles outside of London without his shoes.

At ten minutes past two, Jubal had picked up the key and
removed the painting from the locker. He gave the "detectives" a hundred pounds apiece and hid the van Eyck in his
timber yard. Then he gave the matter some thought. The
painting was catalogued all over the world. No one in his
right mind would try to sell it on the open market. The
obvious thing to do was claim the reward.

To succeed, his plan required certain essentials. The
painting had to be returned and someone had to be arrested for its theft. It didn't have to be the original thief.
Any thief would do. He sounded out Denton. The painting
had been missing for months. There'd been a lot of public-
ity, statements by the police, but no arrest. Denton had
been delighted at the prospect of making an important
capture. Jubal's next step had been to find the victim.
Discreet questioning provided the name of a young Canadian, a dealer of sorts, who lived in Amsterdam, Jamie
Macfarlane. Macfarlane was known to dabble in the odd
painting without asking for a provenance. It seemed that
he had a market in Holland. Jubal let it be known that he
wanted to be informed the next time Macfarlane came to
London. The word came after three weeks. Macfarlane
had arrived and was staying at the Harrogate Hotel in
Bayswater. Jubal had a drink in the hotel bar and identified

the Canadian. The same night he informed Denton and the countdown started.

There had been a box of wigs in the house, something that Millie had brought home from the hairdressing shop. Jubal had chopped one down, wearing it with ankle boots and a sailor's sweater. A pair of Woolworth's spectacles completed his disguise. He arrived in Bermondsey Market shortly after 7 A.M. and stationed himself outside the café, scanning the dealers and public as the crowds passed through the stalls. It was eight o'clock before he located Macfarlane, who was on his own. Jubal made a quick pitch about the painting and the Canadian was obviously interested. Jubal arranged to take the van Eyck to Macfarlane's hotel later on in the day. The next step was to pick up a couple of market runners, men who were used to dubious deals. Neither knew Jubal's real name. He told them what he wanted, gave them twenty pounds apiece and the telephone number of the café. Five hours later, Macfarlane was sitting in a cell in Chelsea Police Station.

Jubal paid off the hack and crossed the short driveway. His wife's Volkswagen was in the garage. He opened the garden door. The one-eyed Doberman came toward him, wagging its stump. A furious banging of drums told him that the twins were somewhere upstairs. He turned the handle of the kitchen door very quietly. His wife was standing with her back to him, looking down into the freezer.

"Gotcha!" he said loudly.

She spun around, her fingers flying to her throat, a slim woman of thirty-five, wearing a fine white-wool dress and too much makeup. Her thick red hair was in shining coils. Shock faded from her face and was replaced with hostility.

"Why do you always have to play the clown? You're worse than the twins, downright childish."

"Get out the smoked salmon," he grinned, running his fingers over her buttocks and goosing her gently. "We're having a party."

She made a show of removing his fingers. Her voice was suspicious. "A party for who? Who's coming?"

"Well," he kidded, his broad smile returning from the mirror in front of them. "I thought we might have Gunilla down. It can't be no fun for her sitting up there night after night watching television."

"Shall I stay or go out?" Millie asked acidly.

He locked an arm around her shoulders. "I'm only joking, doll. But I'm serious about the party. I want you to ask Nell and Sophie over. It's never too late to ask them. Nor too early neither."

Millie closed the lid of the freezing unit. "Just who do you think you are?" she demanded. "Why should I ask people over here to be insulted? Whenever *your* friends come to the house, I'm polite to them. Believe you me, it's not because I *like* them. But at least I'm polite."

"Do as you're told," he said. "Nobody's going to be insulted and I won't even stop Sophie from groping me."

"The trouble with you is that you think everyone else is the same as you are. You're a dirty-minded bastard."

"I don't want to hear that shit," he warned behind uplifted finger. "I'm trying to keep a clean mind in a clean body."

She made a sound of disgust. "All right, what time do you want them here?"

He looked at his watch. "Eight, eight-thirty. We'll have a nice cozy evening, the four of us."

The note of apprehension in her voice came from long experience. "You're not in some sort of trouble, are you, Jack?"

He shook his head, his arm around her waist. "You know

better than that, Millie. I don't *do* that stuff anymore. I just want a nice evening at home. What's wrong with that?"

"Nothing," she said, looking at him speculatively. "It's just that it's been a long time."

They climbed the stairs together. Their field of battle was small and well fought-over. But it was *their* field and *their* battle and no one from outside had any place in it.

4. John Raven

IT WAS WELL AFTER nine o'clock and they were still in the kitchen. The shadows thrown by the candlelight waxed and waned on the ceiling as the houseboat moved on the ebbing tide. The bottle of Krug was empty and they were drinking coffee. Kirstie was wearing a green silk shirt and tan linen skirt. Her legs and arms were sunburned. She was tracing a pattern in the spilled salt by her cup. She looked up suddenly.

"I enjoyed my food. Thank you."

"Thank the Greek," he said, smiling. "I'm a philistine when it comes to food, or so my sister says."

He had spent the first half hour telling her how he had passed the day, explaining about the interviews he had had with Lassiter and Denton, the phone call to the insurance office. She had listened intently, resting her chin in her palm from time to time. She had put only one question to him, asking if he thought that her brother had been framed. He answered honestly. A frame of some kind, certainly. During the rest of the meal, they explored one another gently, talking more about themselves than the events that had brought them together. She had finished school in Switzerland, leaving Leysins fluent in four languages. Her first job was as an interpreter with the United Nations in New York. For the last eight years she had been a free-lance photographer in Paris, working out of an Ile-St.-Louis apartment.

She had tied her hair with a bow at the back of her neck. She looked very tired with violet smudges under her eyes. Tired, lonely, defenseless, and desirable. He reached across the table and placed his hands on hers.

"The night's young. What would you like to do?"

She freed her fingers and found her mirror. It hid her eyes. "What am I being offered?"

He lifted his shoulders. "We've got the car. We could dance if you like, or just listen. There's a place up the river where the pianist plays good jazz."

She closed her handbag. Her lips wore a new gloss. "Couldn't we just stay here?" she asked innocently.

He felt as if he had played an ace to see it trumped. "Absolutely," he said hurriedly. He was amazed to find that he could still blush. "I'll get rid of the plates. Why don't you go into the other room and put on some music? Before I forget it, there's an envelope with some of your brother's things on the desk."

He ran hot water in the sink and dumped the plates in it. By the time he had them back in the drying rack, she was playing a Fats Waller record. Evidently a lady of taste. He blew out the candles and dimmed the sitting-room lights.

"Would you like brandy?"

She was standing by the desk. "Vodka," she said. "You're forgetting."

He fetched the bottle from the refrigerator. She was still at the desk.

"I see you do the whole number," she said, looking down. He filled the two glasses and crossed the room. A drawer in the desk was half-open, showing the butt of the thirty-eight. He closed the drawer.

"Come to think of it, I'm probably breaking the law. I haven't renewed my permit."

They sat on the leather sofa together. The hair at the

base of her neck grew perversely, in soft blond tendrils that reached up like vine suckers. She drank the chilled vodka but kept the glass in her hands.

"Doesn't the thought of breaking the law worry you?"

The malt whisky made a pool of warmth in his stomach. "You wouldn't be here if it did." He smiled, guessing. "You play piano, right?"

"I play piano," she agreed. The movement of her arm released the scent she was wearing. "It's not so unusual."

He refilled her glass. "Not by itself, perhaps. But taken all together you're a pretty remarkable lady."

"Thank you, sir," she said demurely.

He glanced sideways but her smile had no mockery. The record had come to an end. The surrounding houseboats rattled their chains as they rose and fell on the tide.

Her voice was quiet, almost thoughtful. "You really love all this, don't you, John?"

He turned his head slowly and tried to explain. "I'd rather live here than any other place in the world. I can't give you a specific reason. Sure, there are disadvantages. But I know that when I walk down that gangway I leave the world behind me. And most of the time that's a good thing."

"And you're never lonely?" Her second vodka was untouched.

"Sometimes," he admitted. "But not enough to make me change my habits."

"A creature of habit."

"A few that are deeply rooted."

She nodded as if he had just answered a whole string of questions. She frowned as the Great Dane on the neighboring boat started to bay.

"I know him well. He's the one who gets lonely. His master's probably out," said Raven.

"You might as well have a child as a dog," she said suddenly. "In both cases you have to surrender part of yourself."

He flipped the record and sat down close to her. He felt for her hand and found her fingers responsive. He closed his eyes, content for the moment to know that she was there and to be next to her. The Great Dane was baying even louder. Suddenly Raven's grip tightened. His ear detected something unfamiliar in the pattern of sound outside. He freed his hand gently, putting a finger on his lips as he rose to his feet. The dimmed light put the long room partly in shadow. The curtains were completely closed, the door leading out on deck locked. He turned the lights off and put his ear against the crack in the door. Creaks and groans of timber answered the rustle of water. The dog had stopped barking but the noise of drunken singing drifted over the water from the pub on the other side of the Embankment.

"Stay where you are," he whispered. He unfastened the catch very carefully and inched the door open. The deck showed empty in the warm scented night. Lights flashed as cars crossed the bridges. He hooked back the door and stood for a moment, his eyes and ears on stalks. The cedar-wood superstructure ran the length of the houseboat, leaving enough room fore and aft for someone to make the round. The deck was four feet wide on either side, the tubs and flower-holders fastened to the planking. He could neither see, hear, nor smell danger, yet instinctively he knew it was there. He slipped off his shoes and picked up an old winch-handle. His back flat against the curtained windows, he moved away from the open door toward the gangway. The streetlamps overhead bathed the flotilla of boats in a clear light shining on a familiar scene. He padded along the deck, partially reassured and feeling slightly foolish as he completed the circuit. He dropped the winch-handle on a coil of rope and stepped into the sitting room, feeling for the light switch.

"I'm sorry about that . . ." he started, in a normal tone of voice.

Other fingers were quicker than his on the switch. His throat was caught from behind in the crook of an elbow, his body partly lifted off the ground. He hung, choking, in the sudden glare. Kirstie was sitting bolt upright on the sofa, her mouth a slash of red in a colorless face. At her back was a man with yellow curls and an earring. He was holding the open blade of a switchknife against her neck.

A violent shove sent Raven staggering forward. He looked up shakily from hands and knees. The man standing over him was even younger than his partner, with thick black hair and a wet petulant mouth. Tight jeans outlined his legs and he wore pointed boots with brass trimmings. His foot flashed without warning, his toe catching Raven on the temple as he started to rise. Pain spun in Raven's brain, blinding him momentarily. He was on his feet somehow, defending his head with his arms as best he could. The blows thudded home, delivered with the dead weight of fists that were loaded with coins. He felt his eyebrow split. Blood poured down his left cheek. More punches landed on his head, the shock spreading through his skull. He couldn't see his assailant but he could hear the man's labored breathing, the grunt as each blow was delivered. The beating continued for three or four minutes, ending as arbitrarily as it had begun.

A last shove sent Raven sprawling down beside Kirstie. Apart from one cry at the beginning, she hadn't opened her mouth. Raven lifted his forearm, stanching the flow of blood with his shirtsleeve. The man with the earring had moved from behind the sofa and was standing with his back to the deck door. His partner ran a stream of coins from one palm to another and pocketed them. He was breathing heavily and his eyes were very bright.

"Next time it'll be your kneecaps. I felt like being kind today."

He was on the point of saying something else when the phone rang on the desk. The sudden summons dominated the room.

"Answer it!" ordered Raven's assailant.

Raven crossed the room, the man following. Raven picked up the phone, positioning himself so that the inside of the desk was hidden. The voice he heard was his sister's. He spoke very carefully.

"I can't talk now, Anne. I've got people here. I'll call you tomorrow morning."

He put the phone down, grabbing for the gun in the drawer with the same motion. The man stepped back smartly, one arm outstretched as though fending off the shot he expected.

"No!" he said, his face tight and scared.

Kirstie bent down quickly. Then she was on her feet with a shoe in her hand, holding it by the toe. Before anyone could stop her, she swung the shoe viciously, the heel catching the dark-haired man flush in the mouth. He screamed like a stuck pig, holding his mouth with bloodied hands. His eyes were round with disbelief. A car horn sounded outside. Both men turned and ran through the open doorway. Footsteps pounded along the deck, then the car drove off at high speed.

Raven sat down shakily. "They must have followed me round the deck. Bastards!"

Kirstie's fingers were as soft as butterfly wings. She touched his cheek and forehead. The front of her shirt was spattered with blood. More blood was on her heel.

"Why did you let them go?" she demanded.

He looked up, wincing as he grinned, and showed her the empty clip in the gun.

"It wasn't loaded."

Concern gave her a brusqueness that was almost aggressive. "Well, just don't sit there. Come into the bathroom and let me clean you up!"

He followed her in and sat on the edge of the bathtub, telling her where she could find tape, gauze, and antiseptic. She cleaned the blood from his face and eyebrow and held the slit together with her fingers then sealed it with adhesive tape. She dabbed arnica on his swollen temple and stepped back, admiring her work as she dried her hands.

"I've seen a whole lot worse after a hockey game. The edge of a skate can make a slit like that. They usually clamp them but you can always have that done if it opens up again."

He stared in disbelief at his image in the mirror behind her. She made everything sound so normal. She had used the narrowest strip of tape possible and the lump on his temple was smaller than it felt. He glanced down at his trousers. The right leg was ripped from knee to ankle.

"I never did like them anyway. Those two were professionals. It looks as if someone doesn't approve of my interest in Jamie."

He pushed up off the tub, and she followed him into the sitting room. He poured two massive drinks.

"You want to know what triggered this off? I think it was that call to the insurance company. Someone out there is getting nervous."

She caught her upper lip with her teeth, frowning. "The man who claimed the reward?"

He leaned back and closed his eyes. The bright light hurt. "Something like that. We can only guess. The one thing certain is that these people mean business."

"Are you going to the police?"

He saw her through half-closed eyes, a blur and out of focus.

"If the police were any use, Jerry wouldn't have sent you to me."

"I'm thinking about you, not me," she said. "If you wanted to change your mind I'd understand."

He opened his eyes completely. "You mean is my pulse racing and have my knees gone weak? The answer is yes. But I don't like strange hoodlums breaking into my property and busting my face open. No, I'm not changing my mind nor do I need the police."

"I'm glad," she said, without making it clear what she was glad about.

He looked at his wrist watch. The crystal was smashed. "It's getting on to midnight. I'd better call a cab for you. I'm not in the best shape for driving."

She lifted an arm, putting her hand behind her hair. "I'm not leaving. I'm staying right here."

He nodded as if she had just said the most natural thing in the world. He turned his back on her rather than let her see his face. He poured himself a nightcap.

"Then we might as well get some sleep. Your room's the one on the right. You'll find some pajamas in the drawers and a new toothbrush in the bathroom."

He locked the doors, turned out the light, and opened the curtains. There was a sliver of moon on its back over Battersea Park. The Great Dane was silent. Saul was probably home. He brushed his teeth in the bathroom, wincing as the skin on his face stretched. The door to the guest room was closed. But in spite of that, in spite of everything that had happened earlier, there was a feeling of intimacy abroad on the boat and he wondered if Kirstie was aware of it.

She was a stranger in a country where she had few friends. This was odd in a girl with her looks and background, but from what she'd said earlier, his impression was that even in Paris her life was a solitary one. Also odd was the fact that though women had come and gone in his existence, here he was being possessive about a girl he had known for barely twenty-four hours. Deep down he knew that he wanted her to stay on the boat. Maybe it wouldn't work but he had to put it to the test.

He threw his underclothes in the laundry basket and switched off the light. He would tell her in the morning, offer her a bed for as long as she stayed in England. He knew that it was a cop-out but he didn't want to scare her off. He padded across to his bed, naked. As he bent down to pull back the sheet, arms reached for him and he realized that she was lying there in the darkness, waiting for him. Neither spoke, then her lips found his. Her fingers were tender, exploring the secret places of his body until he stirred and rolled over on top of her. They locked together, moving in unison, but pain vanquished his virility and he moved away to lie flat on his back, staring at the ceiling. He felt her turn and guessed that she was looking at him.

"I'm sorry," he said, awkwardly.

Her fingers entwined with his, her voice soft. "It doesn't matter. It'll get better."

He continued to stare at the ceiling. She seemed to have a trick of ignoring his roundabout approaches and cutting to the very heart of the matter.

"Know something?" he said suddenly. "I think I'm in love."

She freed her hand and touched his cheek. "It's happened before. Me too, anyway."

He yawned with an infinite feeling of contentment. This was the beginning of something, not the end. He reached for her quickly, seeking her mouth. It was too dark to see her eyes but he sensed their message.

"Good night, my darling." The words had a strange ring to them but then he was out of practice.

"Tell me something," she said suddenly. "What's all this about a tragedy in your life, some lady? Louise told me."

"Louise talks too much," he answered. It was difficult to find the right thing to say. It all seemed a long time ago. "There was someone, yes."

She made a little growl. "Then I have to tell you this. I've no intention of competing with the ghost of a dead woman."

"You won't have to," he assured her. "There's no room for ghosts."

They lay close, silent until something prompted him to speak. "I'd have helped you in any case, Kirstie. I want you to know that."

"I know it. And I hope you don't think that I sleep with men for favors." Her voice was tart but he guessed that she was smiling in the darkness. They went to sleep with her head on his chest, his arms around her. She was still there when next he opened his eyes. Early daylight pierced the curtains. He freed his arm gently, lowering her head to the pillow. The movement awakened her. She opened her eyes and smiled at him, blond hair snaking across her face. He opened the curtains on a fine cloudless morning.

There was nothing on the river except an eight from a nearby rowing club. Their stroke was ragged and there was a lot of white water. He turned from the window as she swung her long legs out of the bed. Her suntanned naked body showed the marks of the bikini she had obviously worn recently. On a Mediterranean beach, he thought jealously, and wondered who she had gone with. She smiled again, in front of the mirror. There was neither awkwardness nor regret in her manner.

"Hi! Did you sleep well?"

"Like a log." It was true in spite of his injured eye. "How about you?"

She made a circle with her thumb and forefinger and skipped into the bathroom, closing the door after her. He heard the rattle of the shower curtains and then her voice.

"Let me get breakfast!"

He pulled on his pajama trousers. There was a lipsticked handkerchief on the pillow. He stuffed it out of sight, remembering Mrs. Burrows. When Kirstie was through, he followed her into the bathroom. Her mark was already stamped on the things he used every day, the soap left on the upturned nail brush, the toothpaste uncapped. He inspected his eye carefully. The strip of adhesive was still holding the wound together and there was no fresh bleeding. He shaved meticulously, getting the hairs on his Adam's apple. She had remarked on them the previous night.

The kitchen was bright and sunny. Kirstie had plucked some marigolds from the deck. They blazed, true orange, in a vase on the table. Her face was fresh and shining, her hair tied back again with the blue ribbon. They looked at one another across the table, smiling rather than break the spell. There was coffee instead of tea and she had made toast with his wholemeal bread but he didn't care.

"About last night," he said, solicitously. "You must have been scared."

"I was," she admitted. "But for you, not for me. I don't scare that easily."

He bit into the buttered toast, favoring the damaged side of his face. "What's your feeling about Lassiter?"

She pondered her answer, the morning light giving her eyes the brilliance of emeralds.

"I trust him," she said finally. "Yes, I think I do."

"I agree. We may well need him."

She nodded. The coffee they were drinking had been on the boat for months but she had somehow managed to make it taste fresh.

"So what's the next step?" she demanded.

He lifted a shoulder. It was a question he'd been asking himself.

"I'm not sure. I have to give it some thought. But one thing is certain. The action could well get rough. I'd like you to drop out and watch. I want you safe and sound."

She leaned both elbows on the table. "I'm a whole lot tougher than you seem to think, Mr. Raven. I don't just play Beethoven. At Leysins I won the cantonal downhill two years in succession. You happen to be going out with a very tough lady."

"That's not really what I mean," he insisted.

"Then what *do* you really mean?" Her wrists were tanned and strong like her fingers. He imagined her wielding the ski poles as she flashed through the slalom markers.

"Forget it," he said, the right words eluding him.

She collected his cup and plate and washed them up with her own. She was dwarfed in his terry-cloth robe but her movements were quick and positive. She put the crockery in the rack and turned to face him.

"Who looks after you here?"

"Mrs. Burrows." He reached for a cigarette and she passed him the big box of stove matches. "Which reminds me, I'd like to get out of here before she arrives. I don't want a scene."

"A *scene!*" She threw her head back and laughed. "I don't believe it! You mean this lady's going to be temperamental because of me?"

He was finding it increasingly difficult to answer her questions. Difficult and embarrassing.

"She doesn't exactly run my life. She just happens to

think that she should. She had a little trouble with the last lady. Anyway, it's the sort of confrontation I'd rather delay."

Her smile was indulgent. "You mean you don't think that she would approve of me?"

"I *know* she wouldn't," he replied. "These things take time." What he really wanted to know was whether she would be staying. *Kirstie, please stay. I need you.* "She's been with me seven years," he finished lamely.

She pirouetted, sleeves flapping, as she inspected the kitchen. "Well, she's clean at least. Don't worry, darling. I promise that I won't compromise you."

He was on the point of saying that he didn't care, but the lie would have stuck in his throat. The truth was that he wanted Mrs. Burrows to approve, to bend her Cockney loyalty in Kirstie Macfarlane's direction. He moved behind her chair and kissed the nape of her neck. Her flesh had a smell of its own, sweeter than soap and scent.

"You're not angry?" he asked, his lips against her skin.

She twisted in his arms. "You must be joking! I'm intrigued if you like but I'm definitely not angry. In fact I'm rather looking forward to meeting this paragon. Who knows, I might even get her to like me."

"Listen," he said, squatting by her side. "I want you to stay on the boat with me. Let me drive you over to the hotel and collect your things."

"What time does your lady get here? Tell me, I want to know."

"Ten o'clock."

She consulted the thin watch on its striped strap.

"Then we don't have much time. What are your plans?"

"I'm not sure," he admitted. "There are a few things that I have to check."

He followed her into the guest room, sitting on the side of the bed and watching as she put her clothes on. Everything that she did was done naturally, asking him to hook her bra, making him part of the act of her dressing.

"There," she said finally, turning away from the big mirror and smiling at him. "You'd better hurry if you don't want to face your lady. May I have a key?"

He found one for her in the desk. They reversed rooms and roles, Kirstie sitting on the bed as he donned jeans and a blue cotton shirt. He was on one knee, tying the laces of his sneakers, when she made her announcement.

"I'll give your love to Mrs. Burrows, shall I?"

He looked up, startled. "Now what are you talking about?"

She reached down, arranging a lock of his brown-gray hair over his swollen temple.

"You've asked me to stay here with you, right?"

"Right," he agreed and climbed to his feet.

Her mouth kissed without touching him. "Then Mrs. Burrows is just going to have to learn to live with me."

He nodded, relieved that the decision had been taken out of his hands. He left the usual note with some money on the kitchen table and drove Kirstie to South Kensington. He offered to wait and take her back to the boat but she refused. She leaned through the open window and kissed him under the eyes of the hotel doorman.

"I'll see you later, then," she said.

"At home?" There was a good ring to the words.

It was even better when she repeated them. "At home."

His next stop was at a gas station near a bend in the river between Egham and Staines. A peacock was displaying its plumage in the sunshine, safe behind fenced-off grass in front of a timber-built bungalow. Raven touched the horn-button. A boy with a bad case of acne ambled out of the office, a small transistor hanging from a strap on his chest playing tinny music.

"Mr. Karelian around?"

The youth jerked his head in the direction of the bunga-low. Raven backed the Citroën away from the pumps, parked, and stepped over the fencing. The peacock moved away, scolding as Raven made for the pathway. Before he could reach the bell-push, the front door was opened by a man who was made like a Japanese wrestler. The muscles of his body were overlaid with flabby tissue. The fat ex-tended to his face, reducing his eyes to marbles set on each side of a potato nose. He was wearing trousers and sus-penders and Naturfit sandals. The top half of his body was naked, and tattooed across his midriff was the legend

I STAND FOR GOD AND DECENCY

He shut the door quickly behind Raven and led the way into a bright, sunny room with windows overlooking a lawn. Beyond that was the river with swans sailing on it. There was a Blüthner grand piano in an angle of the room with a book of five-finger exercises open on the music stand. A series of very bad flower paintings, expensively framed, hung on the walls. Karelian flapped a hand at a chair and sat down opposite. A head of tight gray curls gave him a vaguely Roman look. He scratched at his left armpit, looking at Raven's face and tutting.

"An inch or so lower and he'd have done your eye in. You want a beer?"

"Yes," said Raven.

Karelian opened a cupboard. There was a small icebox concealed inside. The beer was cold. Karelian drank his from the can. The house was quiet. It was clear that they were alone in it.

"I need your help," Raven said quietly.

The can popped in the other man's hand and Karelian frowned at it.

"You know something, I get pissed off at the way people

are. I mean, nobody ever comes here saying what a great guy Karelian is, let's take him a bottle of Scotch or a box of cigars. No. It's always the other way round. Thieves and rapscallions trying to get something out of a respectable taxpayer."

Karelian's respectability was a subject for debate, founded as it was twenty years before on his share of the airport bullion robbery.

"Did I ever ask you for something for nothing?" Raven inquired.

Karelian widened his mouth and poured the last of his beer down his gullet.

"State your business. I've got my piano lessons to do."

"I need information," said Raven. "Whatever you do, think of it as money in the bank."

Karelian's eyes slid around the room as if searching for something that he had misplaced.

"You're not the law anymore so what sort of information do you want?"

Raven leaned forward, touching his taped eyebrow. The fat man looked hard, as though he had only just noticed the damage. He shook his head commiseratingly.

"I abhor all forms of violence."

"Well," said Raven. "This is what a couple of fag cowboys gave me last night. They broke into my boat and worked me over. Some greasy-haired bastard who uses coins in his hands and a blond with an earring."

Karelian shook his massive head. "Fucking disgraceful. Downright preposterous. What was it all about?"

"I think it was meant to be a warning," said Raven. "The shape of things to come. I want their names, Karelian."

"Ah," said Karelian, and thought about it for a while. "There are hoodlums all over, these days. Kids who'll break your legs for fifty quid. Even less. They nick someone's shotgun, saw off the barrels, and they're in business. There's no discipline anymore. No respect."

"A name," reminded Raven. He described the two men's appearance as best he remembered.

Karelian shook his head. "I don't associate with this sort of person, Raven. You know that. All I can do is ask around. You're not in any . . . I don't know how to put this, exactly."

Raven did it for him. "You want to know if this could be a voice from the past? Someone I put inside and who just got out? The answer's no."

Karelian heaved himself up. "I'll do my best. Are you still living on that barge?"

"Still there," said Raven. "And don't forget. Anything you do for me will be paid for. Discreetly paid for."

5. Smiling Jack Jubal

HE CLOSED the front door on Mrs. Sugarman. She had barely drawn breath for the last two and a half hours but she was already chatting up the black driver of the rented car as they drove away. The last of the Downtown Frolics was still in the drawing room with Millie, drinking brandy and watching television. He took the Doberman and a cheroot out into the garden. The nursery was in darkness but the girl was still up. He fancied his chances there but Millie watched him like a hawk. It was eight months since he'd slept with his wife.

Moonlight and shadow patterned the lawn and the pool. Jubal inspected the dirt round the rose bushes. Mr. Palau did the garden four half-days a week and he strongly disapproved of dog-shit. The Doberman was obstinate in his habits and Jubal had had to take a strap to him. There was a striped-canvas swing at the edge of the pool. Jubal lit his cheroot, sat down, and started rocking himself gently. The dog was scratching around in the bushes.

It would have been a relief if he'd had someone he could confide in but when you came right down to it, he'd been on his own for years. You had to be in his line of business. A nark couldn't afford to have friends. He'd been dead scared in the beginning. He'd grown up in a world where police-informers were marked men, maimed, scarred, and destroyed by the people they betrayed. Some disappeared completely. Scared though he was, he forced himself to put up the front that convinced others and saved him. Good old Smiling Jack, always ready to bankroll a score, buy the odd bit of gear, and, most important, help out a good thief in need. When the squad cars assembled in the first light of dawn, when Old Bill kicked in some villain's door with every dog in the neighborhood barking its head off, Smiling Jack would be in his bed miles away. But he'd be there in the morning, commiserating when he heard the news, and ready with fifty or a hundred toward the defense fund. His confidence grew with his success, peaking when a South London heavy mob came to him for judgment about a betrayal for which he himself was responsible. The decision he made had put another man in hospital with smashed elbows and kneecaps. But that was what it was all about. There were no Queensberry rules in the jungle.

No, the worst of it was having to live your life out like some fucking secret agent, with one cover for this one, another for somebody else. Nobody you could tell the truth to. Millie was useless. She thought she knew the lot but the nearest she got to reality was the suspicion that he occasionally dabbled in hot merchandise. It was expedient for him to let her go on thinking this way.

He put his heel on the stub of his cheroot and whistled up the dog, cursing when it appeared with its usual wolfish silence. The light was out in the *au pair*'s bedroom. It was twenty minutes past eleven. He locked and bolted the kitchen door. The dog slept in the hallway. Voices from the drawing room told him that Millie and Nell Harrigan were still at it. He shut himself in his study. He was proud of his study with its brass-bound desk, shaggy white carpet, and fat leather chairs. He had a set of military prints, Roughead's *Famous Trials,* and four shelves of books. He belonged to two different book clubs. He was happiest in this room with the door securely shut and his feet up on the desk.

The drawer on his right contained the accounts from the timber yard, compiled in a sort of mathematical shorthand that only he understood. He drew the curtains, though the study was at the back of the house. Then he sat down and picked up the telephone. He dialed the code and his own number and replaced the handset. The phone rang ten seconds later. A recorded voice repeated, "Start test. Start test." He put the phone down again. As far as he knew, his number had never been tapped but he believed in taking precautions. The method he had just used was the one employed by Post Office engineers when checking a line. There were four authorities with the power to put a tap on your phone, including the police. But a tap meant a recording device, and only one could be used at any one time. Hearing the engineers' test speech meant that he was in the clear.

He dialed the Bermondsey number. "Dasher? It's me. What news do you have?"

He moved the receiver away from his ear. Dasher's voice was high-pitched and shaking.

"That girl—she's only knocked Eddie's front teeth out and split his mouth wide open, the bitch!"

"Get a hold on yourself," Jubal said sharply. "What happened? What about Raven?"

"Fuck Raven!" screamed Dasher. "Eddie done him over but the bastard pulled a gun. That's when that bitch used her shoe on Eddie's face. Are you listening to me?" he said sharply.

"I'm listening to a whole lot of shit that I don't want to hear," said Jubal. "I'm not interested in Eddie's adventures. I want to hear what he did to Raven."

"He earned his bleedin' money," yelled Dasher. "And you'd better get the rest of it up. Eddie's a good-looking boy and he's going to need taking care of."

"Great," said Jubal. "I've got a feeling that I paid two

hundred quid for a pair of clowns to fuck things up for me."

"You get that money up," said Dasher. "And get it up quick if you know what's good for you!"

Jubal's voice went very quiet. "Don't you dare threaten me, you cocksucker. One more wrong word out of you or those two assholes and you're *all* out of business."

He hung up quickly and reached for the package of Filipino cheroots. It sounded like a shambles on the house-boat but with any sort of luck Raven would have got the message. The news would have to be edited for Denton. He picked up the instrument again and called the number Denton had given him. The Detective-Inspector answered the call himself.

"I took care of that business," Jubal said meaningfully. "I'd say that our friend won't be feeling quite so perky. A lot quieter if you know what I mean."

The line went dead at the other end.

Minutes later, tires sounded on the driveway. The door-bell rang. He heard voices in the hallway, switched off the light, and moved to the curtains. It was Nell Harrigan's rented car outside. He put on the lights again and was back in his seat before the door opened.

Millie's back hair was adrift and she glanced round suspiciously, bright-eyed from the Rémy-Martin she'd been drinking.

"Some sort of a host you are! I don't know why you bother to ask people in the first place. You didn't even bother to say good night to Nell."

He leaned back, grinning. "She wouldn't have noticed anyway. All she ever hears is the sound of her own voice."

Her mouth twisted bitterly. "You don't have a good word for anyone, do you? Even your so-called friends. What makes you think you're so wonderful, anyway?"

There were times when he actively disliked her and this was one of them. He stabbed a finger at her angrily.

"Well, for one thing, putting up with you for eleven years. A little hairdresser's apprentice with two pairs of drawers and four Beatles records. That's what you were when I married you. There were no bleedin' mink coats then, mate. No holidays in Central America. *That's* what I think is so wonderful. It all came from here!" He reversed his finger and touched his forehead with it.

She stifled a belch with the heel of her hand and collected her dignity shakily.

"I'm going to bed," she announced.

"Shut the door behind you," he answered. As soon as she had gone, he unlocked a small cupboard under the built-in book shelves. Inside the cupboard was a panel with switches and a pair of head phones. He thumbed the power on and donned the head phones. Every room in the house was wired, including the bathrooms and lavatories. Electrical engineers had made the installation before Jubal moved in and no one but he knew that it existed. The system had proved invaluable. Drunk or sober, Millie never went to bed without looking in on the twins. He threw the appropriate switch and heard her moving around upstairs, the click as she turned out the lights. Jubal touched a second switch, smiling to himself as he heard the *au pair*'s deep, regular breathing. He'd change all that if he could get into bed with her.

He took off the head phones and locked them away in the cupboard. The Doberman lifted its head from the blanket as Jubal crossed the hallway to the drawing room. Those sluts had left the place looking like a pigsty. The ashtrays were full. There were dirty coffee cups and glasses all over the place, and they hadn't even bothered to put the tops back on the bottles. He carried the cups and glasses out to the kitchen and put a little order in the drawing room. It was good, sitting there with the lights out and the curtains wide. He leaned back on the sofa, a glass of Chivas Regal in his hand, looking out through the windows. The shadows in the garden were deeper, the fat shapes of the trees etched against the sky. He had paid forty-five thousand pounds for the house seven years before. It was worth three times as much by today's values. Then there was the timber yard, no longer just a front but a straight business providing a living for fourteen people. If you added Millie's salon he wasn't far off a quarter-million pounds. Too bloody right, he thought he was wonderful. Nobody else had done it. Nobody else had helped.

His mind returned to Raven. He'd paid three hundred pounds to have something done and they'd fucked it up. That's the way it was these days. You couldn't trust anyone. If those clowns hadn't done a proper job on Raven, the guy could still be a nuisance. Denton had said he was obstinate. Strange, come to think of it, why Denton was so concerned in the first place. With Macfarlane dead they were safe enough. I mean, take his own case. What was he supposed to have done? Claimed a reward and collected it, all perfectly above the law. OK, so he'd given a false name but surely he was entitled to that. A police-informer had the right to protect himself. According to Denton, the insurance company kept its files strictly confidential and in any case there was no connection between George Smith and John Jubal.

He put his glass down, watching the last of the jets wheel in the sky, wing-lights blinking. He was going to have to do something about Millie, sooner rather than later. She could take the twins. You had to give her that, she was a good mother. They had waited seven years to have children, with doctors poking around to see which one of them was infertile. That had been a real giggle. He could have told them all something. Then Millie had gone on hormones and was pregnant in seven weeks. Six months after that, they told her at the clinic that she was carrying twins, no less. Double headaches and two of everything to buy. When he knew that they were boys, he'd wanted to call them Jekyll and Hyde. The names had a great ring to them, Jekyll and Hyde Jubal. But Millie created too much fuss, insisting on Nicholas and Christian. Poor little buggers sounded like hairdressers already.

He plumped up the cushions and let fresh air into the room. Then he stood, as he sometimes did, suddenly afraid, conscious of the terror that stalked him remorselessly even into his dreams. The image was always the same, the Black Maria arriving at the prison entrance. He heard the clang of the gates as they opened and shut. And there waiting in the yard for him would be all the people he had put inside. Only now they *knew* that he had put them inside. Strong hands pushed him out of the prison van, which drove off as he picked himself up. There was nowhere to go. It was a nightmare that he always woke from, sweating.

The phrase whispered in his ear suggestively. *Conspiracy to subvert justice.* But conspiracy with whom? Denton wasn't likely to be stepping forward and you couldn't conspire with yourself. He shook himself free of the haunting fears, irritated by his weakness.

He went upstairs, turning off the lights on his way to the guest room he slept in. His clothes had been moved there and there was no need to use Millie's bathroom. He undressed quickly and got into bed. No, they'd probably hear no more of this Raven. The girl Dasher talked about could well be Macfarlane's sister. It all added up. She was no lady, whoever she was, belting people in the mouth with her shoe. For some reason, the idea made him laugh out loud. He composed himself for sleep, his mind suddenly at rest.

6. John Raven

HE LUNCHED in a pub near the river and spent the next hour in the Reference Room in Chelsea Public Library, finding out as much as he could about Lee, Ungar and Hilary. It was a limited company formed in 1903 and listed in all the professional reference books. A large-scale map located the address in Bayswater. Raven knew the street well, two rows of houses popular with civil engineers and architects who used the premises as offices. He returned the armful of books to the girl at the issuing desk and went out to his car.

He sat for a while in the driver's seat with the roof open, his eyes closed, and the hot sun on his bruised and wounded face. It no longer hurt except when the skin stretched. The attack on him had been no coincidence. It had been meant as a warning that he was treading on someone's toes. *Whose* toes was anyone's guess. One thing was certain. The action supported the suggestion that Jamie Macfarlane had been framed, in all probability so that the insurance reward might be claimed. Macfarlane's suicide must have been an unexpected bonus for whoever was behind the scheme. As far as the law was concerned, the Macfarlane case was closed. The only way now to force an inquiry would be the production of fresh evidence. And that was going to be impossible unless someone broke the rules. He had no illusions about the role he was playing. He

was no knight in shining armor, motivated by any sense of
high moral indignation. He was purely and simply displaying for Kirstie, the action somehow wrapped up in the
word he had used the previous night. Love.

He drove across the park to Bayswater and left the
Citroën on a meter. Then he strolled three blocks west.
The three-story Victorian house was the last in the row and
painted white. Virginia creeper covered the top of the
façade. There was a brass plate on the door. He walked
past with a sideways glance. Some girls were working in the
first-floor office. He followed the wall round into the alleyway, which was hung with ancient ivy. The side door and
embrasure, clogged with dirt and last year's leaves, were
obviously unused. Looking up at the back of the house he
could see men working in their shirtsleeves beyond the
windows.

Success or failure of his plan would depend on what
security precautions the insurance people took to safe-
guard their premises. Firms were usually lax in such circumstances. There was little of value to be stolen, and
whatever cash there was on hand would be locked up in a
safe. Added to which the street was no more than three
hundred yards from Paddington Police Station. He re-
traced his steps to his car. There was nothing more he
could do until nightfall.

Saul Belasus waved from the windows of the Herborium
as Raven backed the Citroën up the alleyway. It was four
o'clock. The river was slack, the paintwork on the *Albatross*
gleaming. He let himself into the sitting room and headed
for the kitchen. That was another thing; he'd have to have
the locks changed. Those thugs must have had a key for
the gangway. His first look was for the back of the kitchen
door. Mrs. Burrows' overall was hanging in its usual place,
which meant that she hadn't walked out on him.

He unlocked the bottom drawer in his desk and took out

the striped sponge-bag that contained his prized collection of skeleton keys and picklocks, the gift of a man long since dead in a prison hospital. He remembered gloves. There was a pair of chamois leather that he sometimes used for gardening. He stripped to his shorts and stretched out on the blind side of the boat, soaking up the sunshine. He heard the clatter of the diesel cab long before it arrived. Kirstie came in, using her key, her heels tapping down the gangway. She must have brought her things on board. She had changed into a blue gauze dress and white loafers. Her brown legs were bare. She bent over and kissed him on the mouth. All his life he'd avoided being kissed on the mouth and now he was enjoying it. She ran her fingers over her blond hair.

"Do you want to hear some gossip?"

He glanced up, shading his eyes from the glare. "If it's scandalous, yes."

"Mrs. Burrows' husband contracted a social disease in Hong Kong when he was in the army. And for years he used to beat her up every weekend but he's stopped now. He's scared of her. And she thinks that you might have come to your senses at last. I'm using her words."

Her face was straight but the glint in her eyes betrayed her amusement. He remembered suddenly that he was supposed to have called his sister but he was in no mood to make explanations. He picked up his clothes and followed Kirstie into the kitchen.

"Does that mean that Mrs. Burrows is staying?" he demanded.

Kirstie looped her canvas bag on the door handle and filled the kettle.

"Of course she's staying. Incidentally, she told me a lot about your ex. In fact, she told me a lot about you in general."

The suggestion put him in mind of her own past, the

apartment on the Ile-St.-Louis, the life he knew nothing about. He changed the subject deliberately.

"What have you been doing all day?"

She poured tea and sat opposite him, holding her cup with both hands, elbows on the table.

"Well, this morning was moving in. I had a snack with Mrs. B. and in the afternoon I went to see Louise. They're both very fond of you, you know."

"It goes both ways," he answered.

She nodded. "I know. And how was your day?"

"Productive," he said. He put his cup down, reached across the table, and took her hands. "I asked a few questions and I learned a few things."

"What sort of things?" The movement of the boat had seemed to worry her at first but now she was used to it.

He eased his grip on her fingers. It was good to feel her skin against his.

"Things about you. Things about myself and about your brother. I'm going to burgle the insurance company's offices as soon as it's dark. I'm pretty certain that's where we're going to find our answers."

Frown lines gathered at the corners of her eyes. *"Burgle?"*

"That's right." He released her fingers and showed her the contents of the striped sponge-bag. "It won't be the first time I've used these things and it probably won't be the last."

She weighed the implements in her palm. "You're full of surprises, my love. You mean you're actually going to break in with these false keys?"

"I was taught by an expert," he answered.

She took the empty cups to the sink. The sun was shining on her hair when she turned her head.

"And what happens if you are caught?"

"I don't intend to get caught," he said calmly. "Neither tonight, tomorrow, nor any other time."

She looked at him for a while, shook her head, and sat down again. "I told Louise about us. That we slept together last night. That I'm in love with you."

"Great," he said, the smile fading on his face. "That must have been riveting for her."

"She's my friend," she said. "And she's your friend, too. She's glad for us, John, and wishes us luck."

"Well, that's something we can use," he answered. "I'm not sure what makes you tick. I mean, a couple of days ago the only thing on your mind was all this about your brother."

Her look was frank and direct. "That was two days ago. I haven't forgotten Jamie but there are two of us to remember him now."

He stretched and faked a yawn, uneasy under the intensity of her look.

"I'm going to take you over to Saul's boat. You can stay there until I get back. I don't want you here alone while I'm gone. It's always possible that we'll have another visit."

"No," she announced. "We're in this together so we share everything, including the risks. I'm coming with you."

He combed his hair with his fingers, pulling it forward over his injured eyebrow.

"OK," he said. "It's against all the rules but practically everything we do from now will be against the rules. Find some gloves and make sure that you leave your handbag behind."

"I'll look for some gloves," she said composedly. "I'm not quite sure what Mrs. Burrows did with them. She unpacked for me."

"That's enough of Mrs. Burrows," he said pointedly. "We can all have a lovely reunion tomorrow morning."

He went into his bedroom to find her nightdress folded on the pillows. She came through the bathroom, swinging a pair of doeskin gloves from her fingers.

"This is really getting exciting. I always wanted to be a burglar, ever since I read *Jimmy Valentine, Amateur Cracksman!*"

He looked round from the mirror. "No wonder you're lacking in respect for law and order."

She ruffled the hair he'd just tidied and took his arm. "I snooped around this morning, but there are things that you have to show me. I want to know about your paintings, your books, and your records. I want to know *why*."

They spent an hour going through the book shelves and his record collection. She announced that she didn't like the Klee or any kind of abstract painting. Later on, he made Pimms in tall glasses while she cooked ham, eggs, and French fries. When they had eaten they sat on the sofa and listened to Beethoven.

"Do you like me?" Raven demanded suddenly.

Kirstie raised her eyes from the magazine in her lap. "What are you, a child? What a funny thing to ask."

He shook his head obstinately. "You don't necessarily have to like in order to love. It's not the same."

She inspected him carefully, like a botanist confronted with an unknown species. She gave him a smile that was both affectionate and compassionate.

"We like you fine. But we're of the opinion that most of all we love you. We think."

"You only think?"

"That's right," she said. "As my father was wont to say, 'when you're sure you can never be certain.'"

"Your father sounds like a muddled thinker," he retorted.

Her eyes left him, traveling to a secret destination. "We'll see," she said composedly.

By the time they reached Hyde Park Square, the street-lamps were already lit, the night suffused with summer's soft gray and lavender. It was a neighborhood popular with Arabs. Rolls-Royces decorated with sheaves of parking tickets stood outside front doors controlled by television cameras. Chauffeurs hawked and spat and the curtains in the houses remained permanently closed. Raven left the car near the church, switched off the motor, and pulled on his gloves. Kirstie followed suit, smoothing the soft skin over her fingers and smiling.

"You're the expert but if I was a cop I'd run you in on sight. A man wearing gloves in the middle of summer?"

"You're *not* a cop," he replied, irked by the criticism. "And I keep my hands in my pockets." The keys and picklocks were hard and flat against his hip. They were no more than a couple of hundred yards from the insurance company's offices.

He opened his door. "Act naturally," he warned. "We're looking for this Malay restaurant some friends told us about."

She tucked her arm under his and matched his stride. He tightened his biceps, enjoying their closeness. They turned the corner. The brick façades of the houses were mellow in the light from the streetlamps.

"The end house," he said. "And don't look round."

They climbed three steps and she stood behind him as he lifted the door knocker. There were two locks, a mortise and a spring-cup lock. He ran a strip of mica down the crack in the door. It passed below the level of the mortise keyhole. That meant that only the Yale was in use.

"Someone's coming," Kirstie said hurriedly. "A man and a woman."

Raven heard the approaching footsteps and lifted the door knocker again. The noise echoed inside the house. "They've gone," Kirstie said quietly.

Raven produced his Yale master keys. He opened the door at the second attempt. They moved quickly into the dark hallway and he closed the door behind them. The house was completely still. There was little sound from the street, none at all from the house next door. Light from a nearby streetlamp shone through the transom over the front door, laying a pattern across the dark green carpet. Raven thumbed up the catch, preventing a key from being used on the outside. Stone steps descended from a door at the back of the hallway to the garden. He crossed neat grass to the door in the ivy-encrusted wall and drew the bolts. If they did have to run for it, the car was only a couple of minutes from the end of the alleyway.

Kirstie was waiting in the hallway. Graceful when moving, she was awkward in repose. He thumbed back at the garden.

"That's our escape route!"

She smiled. "*Alias* Jimmy Valentine."

He closed the garden door. "What?"

"Forget it," she said.

The two rooms leading off the hallway were open. "Stay here," he instructed. "And keep your voice down if you have to speak."

She watched from the shadows as he rummaged through drawers and files. It took no more than a couple of minutes for him to realize that he was wasting his time. He fared no better in the neighboring office, finding only a battery of dictating machines linked to electric typewriters. Kirstie followed him up the stairs to the second floor. The board room was furnished in gleaming mahogany with somber portraits of the whiskered founders hanging on the walls. The only other room on the floor was a kitchen. They climbed to the next floor, lighted by Raven holding the pencil flash. Kirstie stayed close behind, occasionally grabbing at the nearest part of his clothing. Neither spoke. The top landing was painted white. The handles and locks on the doors were made of brass. The narrow beam from the flash traveled over a wide-topped desk and chair. There were shelves of books dealing with law, insurance, and actuarial procedure. Raven pulled a few drawers at random, closing the last with a presentiment of failure.

"I've got a feeling that we've blown it," he admitted. "That we've picked the wrong place. The records are probably kept somewhere else."

He snapped off the flashlight. Kirstie's voice came from the sudden darkness.

"Can't you remember the number you called?"

"Sure." He fished the piece of paper from his pocket.

"Then check the phones," she suggested.

The flash came on again. There were two telephones on the leather-topped desk. Neither number was the one he had called previously. He opened the room next door and hit the jackpot. This number was the one that he wanted. The beam of light touched on a picture of a woman with a child, a personal telephone book with a red star pasted on the cover. The letters in the wire basket were addressed to Mr. H. Kent, Claims Officer.

It was a large room with one wall entirely lined with tall metal filing cabinets. A number was stenciled on the front of each cabinet. Near the window was a scanning machine with a tape and a magnifying screen. He switched this on. The title headings on the screen were in alphabetical order. He ran the tape back to M and sharpened the focus, looking for Macfarlane. The name didn't appear on the tape.

He was luckier with EYCK, PETER van. The screen referred him to file 10(c). He turned to Kirstie, all the old thrill of the chase in his voice. *"Banco!"*

She had been watching over his shoulder and was ahead of him to the row of filing cabinets. She yanked a door.

"It's locked!"

He used one skeleton key after another and the pick-locks. They were all too big to fit in the tiny lock. He looked up, frustrated.

"Isn't that typical? We could walk into a bank with this equipment but a rubbishy lock like this . . ."

He mopped his face delicately. Salt sweat was getting under the tape on his eyebrow and stinging.

"I'll have to break it open," he said. "It's the only way."

He looked around but could see nothing that might serve. He found what he wanted hanging on the staircase, a cavalry saber in its scabbard. He unsheathed it and ran back upstairs. Kirstie watched, hand over her mouth, as he inserted the blade in the cabinet. It snapped at the first try, two-thirds breaking off. He shoved the shortened weapon in the crack and wrenched the heavy hilt. The lock cracked like a revolver shot and the filing cabinet was open. There were six drawers inside, each nine inches deep. He pulled the third from the top and lifted out a small cardboard box. On it was a label that read

EYCK PETER van—MACFARLANE JAMIE— SMITH GEORGE

Raven held the pencil flash in his teeth so that his hands were free. Inside the box was a plastic folder with several objects. Half a dozen snapshots taken with a 35mm camera, all of the same man taken from different angles. The negatives were there, a print of a thumb and forefinger and the Japanese felt pen they must have been lifted from. The last item was a receipt for eleven thousand, two hundred pounds in cash and written on the assessors' official stationery. The signature was in a clumsily disguised hand. *George Smith.*

Raven removed the flash from his mouth and sat back hard on his heels, grinning.

"How about that?" he demanded triumphantly. "Can you see what these monkeys have done?"

She moved the flash so that she could inspect the photographs. "I'd say they used a hidden camera, in all probability automatically controlled. But I wouldn't think that it would do them much good. That guy's wearing a wig if ever I saw one and look at the spectacles! I doubt if his own mother would recognize him."

"She won't be asked to," said Raven, reading the rest of the receipt. "We've just had our first break. You can bet the address the man's given is false but fingerprints don't lie. And he just might have a record." He put the articles back in the plastic container and stuffed this in his pocket. He rose to his feet.

They ran downstairs to the hallway. Kirstie grabbed his arm. "What about the back door? Hadn't you better lock it?"

He shook his head. "There's no point. They're going to know that someone's been here in any case."

He watched from the front window until he was sure that the street was clear. They left the house hurriedly. Minutes later they were sitting in the Citroën. Kirstie started to laugh and turned to him, exultant. "We *did* it, John! Hey, was I good?"

"Brilliant," he said. "If we ever run out of money we know what to do!"

She shook her head in disbelief, looking down at her hands. "Would you believe it, I've just started to shake."

He turned the ignition key, bringing the motor to life. "There won't even be an alarm until morning. Relax."

Traffic along the Embankment was still heavy. She clung to him tightly as they crossed the street to the river and he guessed what was on her mind.

He spoke with false conviction. "They won't be back

tonight. But you can expect some reaction when they hear what's happened. It just might make them show themselves."

Her loafers rattled on the gangway planks. "Couldn't you ask for police protection?"

He glanced back over his shoulder. "Who needs it? I've got a lady who takes off her shoes and steams into action."

"But seriously," she insisted.

"No," he said. "It's the one thing we can't afford to do. We have to keep well away from the police until we've got the sort of evidence even they can't ignore."

The river seemed quieter than usual. The smell of stock and wallflower was heavy on deck. He unlocked the sitting-room door. When he closed and bolted it, she was looking at him curiously.

"This hostility to the police, I don't get it. After all, you were a cop yourself."

He pressed the button, drawing the curtains. "That's why. It doesn't take long to get where you've been."

She untied the ribbon and shook her hair free. "I feel like a drink after all that excitement. I'll get some ice."

He emptied the plastic envelope onto the table and looked at its contents again. These were very hot properties and he had to find a safe place to hide them. He loaded his thirty-eight and checked the safety catch. Ice chinked against glass. Kirstie came in, using a crystal vase as an ice bucket. Women usually respected the private factor in other people's homes far more so than men but Kirstie had done everything as though she belonged, right from the start. A very special sort of lady, he thought. Positive without being pushy, sensual rather than sexy. In fact, *his* kind of lady.

She returned with the glasses and poured herself a vodka. "What may I fix you, my love?"

"Scotch-and-water, please. No ice."

She brought him his drink and sat down next to him on the sofa. She smoothed her hair from her face.

"Here's to crime! Are you any good with that thing?" She pointed at the gun on the table.

"The world's worst," he admitted. "But you're the only person who knows it." Their smiles locked for a moment and then he took the plunge. "I'd like you to tell me the truth about something, Kirstie."

She buried her nose in her glass, studying the expression on his face. "That sounds like a loaded request but I'll give it a try. Go ahead."

"It's about your boyfriends." His neck reddened as her smile grew wide. "The men in your life."

"Oh *that!*" she said. "For a moment you had me worried. There were only two and I made the same mistake with them both. I'm trying desperately not to make it again."

He swallowed his drink. He was pretty sure that he was making a fool of himself but by now he was committed. "What mistake was that?"

Her eyes were suddenly serious. "As a little girl I loved and admired my father. I used to measure my sweethearts against him, even then. So when I grew up I had these preconceived ideas about the way my boyfriends should live and be. It didn't work out, of course. The better I knew them, the more disillusioned I became."

He leaned his head back on the velvet cushion. "That doesn't sound too promising for me."

She reached across and put her lips against his cheek. "You simply are not listening. I just said that I'm not making the same mistake a third time. Besides, you're different."

"I am?" He turned the corners of his mouth down. "What nationality were the others?"

She made a mock gesture of despair. "Men!" The next thing you'll ask is if they were good lovers. One was Canadian, the other French. Both of them admitted to being handsome, charming, and highly intelligent. I'm going to take a shower. Hurry up and come to bed, please." She took the glasses through to the kitchen.

The phone rang before he could follow. It was his sister. He excused himself quickly. "I called earlier but there was no answer."

"I had to take the children for their dental checkup. Has George Ashley been in touch with you about these shares?"

Their lawyer had been in touch a week ago. It suddenly seemed a very long time. "Yes, he has," he said.

"What did you decide to do?"

"I took his advice and signed."

"That's what I was going to do," said his sister. "But Jerzy isn't too happy about it."

The thought of his brother-in-law, a dedicated socialist, intruding in what was strictly a family affair irritated Raven. He frowned. "What does he want you to do with the shares, sign them over to Amnesty International?"

Anne's voice thinned appreciably. "There's absolutely no need to be insulting, John. I simply called to find out what you had done. After all, I have the children to consider."

Even as a child she had used non sequiturs freely as a means of changing the conversation.

"Consider them by all means," he answered. "And sign George's proxies. Look, Anne. It's getting late and I have someone here."

"I know," she said tartly. "Mrs. Burrows called me this morning. I hope you know what you're doing. It's about time you did!"

The sound of Kirstie singing in the shower only added to his sense of outrage. "Wait a minute!" he said hotly. "Are you telling me that my cleaning woman called you to discuss my private affairs and you actually *listened* to her?"

Her tone was sisterly and indulgent. "Don't be childish,

John. It wasn't like that at all. After all, Mrs. Burrows is very fond of you and quite naturally assumed that I was *au courant*."

"That you were what?" he repeated, baffled for the moment.

"*Au courant*," she repeated. "I'm looking forward to meeting the lady. She's an American, I understand."

"Canadian," he repeated mechanically.

"Isn't it the same?" his sister asked sweetly. "You must bring her over for a drink. Good night, John, and thanks for the advice."

The bathroom was free, the soap left in the bottom of the tub. The big bath towel smelled strongly of Kirstie's scent. He brushed his teeth and switched off the light. Her arms reached out from the bed to welcome him and this time their lovemaking was complete. They lay exhausted, staring at one another in the half-light. She touched his face with her hands.

"Good night, my darling."

"Good night," he said. He was still trying to see into her eyes when sleep overtook him.

7. Smiling Jack Jubal

THE PREMISES of Godhawk Timber and Sawmills sprawled on the edge of a hundred acres of wasteland littered with rusting car bodies. A nearby dump had subsided, the cavity filling itself with a noisome scum-topped body of water in which dead cats floated. The wind from the west in summer was objectionable. The timber yard, sawmill, and offices were built on the only really solid ground in the area and connected with the busy highway by a hard-topped service road.

Jubal was in the small two-story brick block overlooking the seasoning sheds. His room was on the first floor and there was little in it. A desk, chairs, a couple of telephones, and a locked closet in which he permanently kept a complete change of footwear and clothing. There were two doors. One opened into the corridor, the other into the yard, enabling Jubal to come and go, unnoticed by the girls in the neighboring rooms.

Ned Granger, the manager, doubled as foreman and spent more time handling timber than correspondence. He was a nonsmoking teetotaler who was dedicated to wood and his work. He was on a good salary and a ten percent profit bonus. He accepted Jubal at face value and kept Godhawk Timber in the black.

Jubal was sipping tea at the open window, the door to the corridor locked and his shoes off. A heat haze hung over the sour derelict land beyond the barbed-wire fence that surrounded the sawmill. He turned quickly, making a long arm as the phone rang behind him. The number was not in the directory and was known only to a few people. To reach him, Millie had to go through the switchboard in the corridor. The caller was Denton.

"There's a pub called the Goat and Compass in the mews behind Kensington Square. Be there at half-past eleven!"

Jubal glanced at his wrist automatically. It was five to eleven and he was six miles from Kensington. He started to remonstrate but Denton cut him short.

"Just *be* there!" he said and hung up.

Jubal refilled his cup. The tea was lukewarm but he didn't notice it. He took the trees out of his snakeskin loafers and eased his feet into them carefully. Denton must have somehow heard what had happened on the boat the previous night.

Jubal left the Jaguar in the National Car Park and walked south across Kensington Square. Children were playing on the grass behind the protective railings, well-dressed children with loud assured voices guarded by long-legged women. A night's rest had done nothing to lessen his dissatisfaction with Millie. The twins and the *au pair* safely out of the way, he and Millie had really gone at it across the breakfast table, resurrecting all the old arguments and airing a couple of new ones. He grinned as he remembered the final exchange. He'd told her that he was going to leave her. She had pushed her chair back, her face stony.

"What about the twins? Don't you care that they'll have no father?"

"They'll get used to it," he'd said with a wave. "In any case I'll see them from time to time."

"I'll kill myself," she announced with a tragic stare.

He shook his head. "Not you "

She thought for a moment. "Then you'll have to give me half of everything. The timber yard, the house. Everything. All done through lawyers."

"That's different," he'd said quickly. "What's for supper?"

He could smile now but when the moment was right she'd have to go.

The pub was at the end of the mews, a small tavern built when the "bijou residences" were still homes for coachmen and horses were stabled in the garages. There were two bars. The bigger was empty. Denton was waiting in the Snug, a tiny room with two booths. Jubal bought himself a glass of tonic water and carried it across. He sat down, smoothing the tow-colored hair over his ears. Denton's face told him nothing.

"This is getting to be a habit," Jubal said, smiling.

Denton leaned back against the oak partition, eyes narrowed as he took in Jubal's elegance. He himself was wearing a red-striped shirt without a tie. The barmaid was talking to a man who had followed Jubal in. Denton's voice was quiet.

"The insurance company's offices were broken into last night. Only one thing was taken—a file. Do you want to know what was in it?"

Jubal wet his lips with the tonic water. "What?"

"Well," said Denton, cocking his foxy head. "It seems that George Smith didn't make too good an impression on the people over there. In fact they felt that there was something very phony about him."

Jubal reached for a cheroot. "What about the file?"

"All in good time," said Denton. "I'm telling you what the man in Claims said when he called me at five past nine this morning. It seems that they noticed the wig and the glasses didn't inspire much confidence."

"So?" Jubal brushed a hand through the cloud of smoke. "A man's entitled to pertect his interests."

"Exactly," said Denton. "I couldn't have put it better. That's really what this meeting is about, protecting one's interests. That's what the insurance people did. They took your picture with a hidden camera and lifted your prints from the pen you used to sign the receipt. That's what was in the file. Prints, receipt, photographs and negatives. All gone."

Jubal shook his head, trying to think. "Raven?"

"Naturally," said Denton. "First of all he goes to see Macfarlane's lawyer, collects some things for the sister, and then pumps the insurance company for information. Who else but Raven? You must have done a great job on him last night."

The back of Jubal's neck was sticky. He tried to ignore the fact that there were more important things to think about than the previous night's fiasco.

"Why did the insurance people get in touch with you?"

Denton took his thumb and forefinger from his nose. "Two reasons. One, *I* was the arresting officer. Two, *I* vouched for George Smith as being the man entitled to claim the reward. That's all I know about him really. Just another police-informer. The local police have been informed."

Someone fed a coin to the jukebox. "So what's the position?" Jubal asked.

"Ah!" He leaned a little closer. "I talked to the officer investigating the break-in at St. Michael's Street. They get a dozen a day, this kind of complaint, meatball raps that involve little or no loss to property. They don't have the men or the time to chase them up."

The news put Jubal in better heart. He took his glass to the bar and added gin and ice to the tonic water.

"So there's really nothing to worry about," he said, sitting down again. "The address on that receipt is a phony and the prints won't do him any good. I don't have a record."

Denton nodded. "That's the way it looks. I'm happy for you, Smiler. As of twelve o'clock noon you and I are parting our ways. No more meetings, no more business together. Finished."

Denton's total defection left Jubal feeling as if he'd been sandbagged. "If I'd been smart," he said bitterly, "I wouldn't have come within fifty miles of you in the first place."

Denton opened a silver cigarette case and stuck a smoke in his mouth. "But you're *not* smart! You never have been smart. You're one of those big fat roaches that's afraid of the light and smells of shit. A common or garden nark." He came to his feet, keeping his back to the bar so that only Jubal could hear what he said. "I want no trace of petty revenge, paranoiac behavior, or base ingratitude. Life is real and life is earnest." He nodded pleasantly and went out into the mews.

The blare from the jukebox stopped abruptly. The barmaid completed her anecdote. Jubal shoved his glass across the counter.

"Stick a large gin-and-tonic in there."

The jukebox music was still playing inside his head. He carried the drink back to his table and sat as far back as he could. He had always figured that under pressure Denton would dump him. But the way it had been done was brutal, with the insults and all, as if he was some creep without any standing. He'd put a dozen captures in Denton's way, every single one of them making the headlines—with "Denton The Hammer" standing in court trying to look modest as some stupid judge banged on about Denton being "a credit to the Force." Some credit!

Jubal reviewed his position. He had fronted all kinds of

insurance companies. Fourteen times, he'd done it, without running into any sort of trouble until this happened. The law supplied a letter that identified you as the informer responsible for the return of the stolen property and the companies paid up. It was as simple as that. The business with the wig and the spectacles was normal. He had always rung the changes on his appearance. And now this. Taking his picture and fingerprints no less! But so what? He had no police record.

The old fear returned with its insidious suggestion. Suppose Raven got to know who Jubal really was and, through Raven, everyone else. Jubal felt that he was being harassed by a prick with the need to fuck in other people's affairs. And the man wasn't even a cop anymore, just a smart-assed bastard doing his number to impress the Macfarlane girl. What kind of system was it where a man ran grave risks to help the enforcement of law and order only to get harassment from the likes of this Raven? Jubal tried to conjure up a picture of the man. To start with, he had to be some kind of freak. Who'd live on a boat that never went anywhere? Only a lunatic who saw himself flying all over the place like Batman, putting down evil.

Jubal lit the cheroot that had been hanging from his mouth for the last five minutes. Raven had his picture, his fingerprints, and the receipt he had given the insurance people. They would probably be on the boat. Jubal's uneasiness intensified. He had a vivid impression of the evening newspaper with block headlines screaming the news.

SUPER NARK IDENTIFIED

John Jubal, 35, spoke to our reporter from behind a locked door late last night . . .

Jubal stubbed the cheroot out hurriedly, as if the lighted end were in his mouth. The more he thought about it, the clearer he perceived that his problem was with Raven. The equation was simple. Remove Raven and there would be no more problem. It would have to be done cunningly. No mercenaries this time, no one to fuck it up or betray him. An hour's work and his troubles and fears would be over. He had no intention of retiring. He had too good a thing going for him. He could always move on from Denton.

He left the pub and walked to Kensington Square. Twenty minutes later he was buying a pair of ex-Luftwaffe binoculars in a secondhand store on Praed Street. He drove south, parked the Jaguar, and walked back over Battersea Bridge. The sun was high in a cloudless sky, the water below sparkling. Jubal hung the strap around his neck, perched his elbows on the parapet, and focused the binoculars. The flotilla of boats stood out sharply, etched against the background. A wartime motor torpedo boat, a river cruiser with a decided list to starboard, a genuine Upper Thames houseboat with striped lifebuoys and dinky little curtains, a couple of converted barges, and the last boat of all, moored at the end of the line. He could read the name painted on the stern, ALBATROSS. There was a long superstructure with large windows, a television mast, and flowers growing all over the place. He could detect no movement on board. A gangway with handrails connected the boat with a flight of steps cut in the Embankment and was sealed with a door hung with barbed wire.

Jubal put the binoculars back in their case, walked to the north side of the bridge and strolled past the *Albatross*. The superstructure was made of cedar planking and tiles. He could see through the big windows into an enormous living room. There was still no sign of anyone. A freak with a beard was leaning over the rail of the lopsided pleasure steamer, watching a Great Dane swimming in the river below.

Jubal had a meal in a Battersea pub and spent the afternoon between a bench in the park and the foreshore below. From time to time, he climbed down to a stone parapet that was a couple of feet above the water. From there he could see under the two bridges, clear across the river to the boats moored in the reach. It was four o'clock when he first spotted movement on the *Albatross*. A tall man with longish hair was taking off his jeans and shirt and lying down on the deck, face to the sun. Jubal kept the boat under observation. Half an hour or so later, a good-looking girl descended the stone steps and let herself through the door at the end of the gangway. The man rose to meet her and they embraced. Then he picked up his clothes and they both went inside.

Jubal lowered the binoculars. He'd seen all he needed to see for the moment. Raven was sporting a patch or something on his left eyebrow and the girl was definitely Macfarlane's sister. They had the same nose and the same color hair. Jubal climbed back over the coping and returned to his car. He moved it out of the area, driving north to Soho, where he spent the rest of the evening. He ate an indifferent meal, complained about it, and saw a skinflick. At eleven o'clock he called Raven's number. A voice with an upper-class accent answered. Jubal made a wong-number excuse and hung up. It was shortly after midnight when he unlocked the gate leading to the timber yard. The office building was dark and silent. The wood in the seasoning shed glimmered where moonlight slanted in.

Jubal drove the Jaguar into the shed that housed the two five-ton timber trucks and the manager's Volkswagen. The teetotaler was a lay preacher whose mission took him forty miles out of London every Tuesday evening. He traveled by train, leaving his Volkswagen at the timber yard for the night. A prudent man, he kept a spare set of ignition keys

in a magnetized holder clamped under a fender. Jubal
retrieved it. He filled two five-gallon cans with gasoline
from the fuel pump outside and put them on the back seat
of the Volkswagen together with cotton waste. Ten minutes
past midnight. He drove along the service road and turned
east toward the river.

He left the Volkswagen fifty yards from Albert Bridge
and climbed over the coping again. Night and the moonlight on the water made it necessary for him to readjust the
binoculars, but he managed to produce a sharp image of
the boats moored in the reach. The *Albatross* was in darkness except for one curtained window aft on the river side.
He concentrated on this but there was no sign of movement behind it. Suddenly the light went out. He put the
binoculars down. There was a slight breeze coming off the
water but Jubal was sweating. He was over the parapet and
under the trees when a man stepped from the shadows
onto the pathway. He was decently dressed, in his fifties,
with an ingratiating manner. His voice was educated.

"A beautiful evening. Were you studying nature?"

He was standing in the middle of the pathway so that
Jubal would have to step round him. There was an emana-
tion of heat from his body and a strong smell of scent.

"Piss off!" Jubal said brusquely.

The man attempted to grab him by the arm. "Don't go!
Please don't go."

Jubal wrenched his arm free and struck the man in the
face with the heel of his hand. There was a sound of pain
and the man staggered away, holding his mouth. Jubal
looked back from the shelter of the Volkswagen, the
adrenalin running in his veins. The brief violence had
calmed him in a strange way. The night-walker had totally
disappeared. Jubal started the motor, drove across Albert
Bridge, and made a left. Fifty yards on, he stopped. The

stone steps leading down to Raven's boat were directly on
his flank. Jubal cut his lights. Traffic flicked by in both
directions but pedestrians were few. He opened the near-
side door and carried one of the five-gallon cans to the
bottom of the steps. The door at the end of the gangway
was locked. Chains attached the boat to massive rings em-
bedded in the masonry. Truck tires served as buffers. The
barbed wire festooning the top and sides of the door made
it difficult to climb onto the twelve-foot gangway. The
Albatross rose and fell on the current, the gap between the
hull and retaining wall widening and narrowing. The deck
was tantalizingly close. Jubal could smell the flowers
strongly. The superstructure was thirty yards long and half
as wide. Drawn curtains made it impossible to see through
any of the windows. The window where he had seen the
last light was on the other side of the boat. There were two
ways of getting on deck—climbing over the wire or dropping down from the stone wall along the Embankment.
You'd be dead if you missed your footing, your skull
crushed between the boat and the retaining wall. Traffic
had eased to the occasional passing of a truck or car. Footsteps came and went but still Jubal did nothing. He was still
sweating but perfectly calm. A pattern of creaks and clanks
from the boat had established itself, enormous sighs as the
truck tires took the weight of the *Albatross.* Moonlight illuminated the motley collection of boats, giving them the
stillness of a film set where unattended cameras await the
actors.

Jubal uncapped the can of gasoline and leaked its contents under the door. At the end of the gangway, the liquid
ran freely, soaking into the planks. The empty can hit the
surface of the water, filled and sank. Jubal ran up the steps,
grabbed the second can, and a handful of cotton waste. He
hoisted the can up on the wall. There was no one to see as

he spilled the contents over the deck below. He moved as he poured, hitting both deck and the roof of the super-structure. The second container sank without trace. He put a match to the two pads of soaked waste and flung them hastily, one at the deck below, the other at the gangway. A second later, the boat erupted in flames. Jubal ran for the Volkswagen. The last thing he heard as he drove off was the baying of a large dog.

It was one o'clock by the time he returned to the timber yard. He drove the Volkswagen into the shed and put the keys back in their hiding place. His clothes stank of gaso-line. He let himself into his office and changed into the slacks and shirt that were hanging in the closet. The others could go to the cleaners in the morning. He closed the big gates of the yard behind the Jaguar and drove home with the radio playing, his fingers tapping out the rhythm on the steering wheel. The Doberman greeted him silently, ramming a wet nose at his hand and wagging its stump tail. Jubal poured himself a large Glenfiddich and carried it upstairs. A crack of light showed under his wife's bedroom door and he heard her call to him.

"Is that you, Jack?"

He switched off the lights on the landing, his voice sar-castic. "Were you expecting someone else?"

He guessed that she'd be sitting up in bed glaring at the door.

"Where've you been?" she demanded.

"Stocktaking," he answered.

"Liar," she said bitterly.

He closed his door on her and got into bed, sipping his Scotch and staring at the open window. Millie would have to go with the kids. A lot of his feelings about them were assumed, a charade played for himself and intended to show that he was a good father. The truth was that he cared for them slightly more than he cared for the dog. Millie could go. The kids could go and so could Denton. He'd proved tonight that nobody fucked with Jubal. Other people didn't have to know it. *He* knew it and that was what mattered. He fell asleep with the crackle of flames in his ears.

8. John Raven

HE WOKE SUDDENLY, rising in the bed and pressing down hard against the mattress. He was aware of danger, detecting its presence with all his senses. He could hear the furious barking of the Great Dane and he could smell smoke. A ruddy light flickered across the window and the taste on his tongue was acrid. Kirstie was still asleep, one arm thrust over her head. He threw himself out of the bed, yanking the sheet and blanket with him as he went.

"Fire!" he yelled. He threw his toweling robe at her, jumped into his trousers, and dragged her into the sitting room. He stabbed at the curtain control and the motor whirred, releasing the velvet drapes. A solid sheet of flame showed outside, cracking the window panes even as they looked. Raven wrenched open the door leading out on deck. "Blankets!" he shouted.

Kirstie ran barefooted into the bedroom and came back with an armful. Her eyes searched his but she showed no sign of panic. They ran to the end of the boat. Flames and smoke engulfed the whole starboard deck. The cedar tiles were burning and the gangway had completely disappeared. They could hear the dog still baying frantically, the shouts from the other boats. Then the clanging of a fire engine shattered the night. Raven and Kirstie beat at the flames with the blankets. Fragments of burning wood were landing on Raven's naked back and chest. Someone shouted from above and he looked up. A helmeted head was leaning over the wall.

"Back!" yelled the man. "Get the hell out of it! Stand well back!"

Raven took Kirstie's hand and ran her to the sheltered side of the boat. High-pressure jets of water hit the fire. The deck vibrated under the impact. The conflagration was under control in a matter of minutes. Someone turned a valve and the brass nozzles of the slack hoses dropped, clanking against the granite retaining wall. Pieces of burned rope floated below and the surface of the water was oily and iridescent. Raven kicked the wet dirt from his bare feet. A number of things were going through his mind at the same time, among them the thought that Kirstie was half-naked.

"Are you burned?" he asked quickly.

Her face was smudged, the blond hairs on her forearms singed where she'd rolled up the sleeves of the toweling robe. She shook her head.

"Go inside," he instructed. "I'll handle this."

She went without argument. The starboard side of the houseboat was a shambles, the walls of the superstructure deeply charred. The force of the jets had overturned flowerpots and tubs, spilling dirt and plants in a muddy wash that slopped about with the movement of the boat. Intense heat had released the brewery smell of the timbers, but over and above everything hung the pungent stink of gasoline. Raven looked up, shading his eyes. The searchlights on the fire engine were extinguished. The same man shouted down again.

"Your gangway's gone. How can we get down?"

Raven pointed at the neighboring boat. "Take the next set of steps!" He put a plank from one boat to the other, crossed it, and grabbed the Great Dane by the collar. Saul

Belasus emerged from the wheelhouse wearing a striped nightshirt. His head was cocked on one side as if listening but the voices he heard were not of this world. "It's the fuzz," said Raven. "Get Herbie below!"

Two men came down the stone steps, a fire officer in a helmet and a uniformed patrol cop. The fire officer clambered aboard, moving awkwardly in heavy protective clothing and boots. He pushed his helmet up, pointing at the *Albatross*.

"Are you the owner?"

Raven nodded. "John Raven."

The fire officer's face was serious. "Well, let me tell you that you're a very fortunate man. A cabdriver saw the blaze and called the alarm. The fire couldn't have been going for long. We were here in seven minutes."

"Brilliant," said Raven. Blood was running down his cheek. The tape had come off his eyebrow and the cut had reopened.

The fireman fished in a pocket and came up with a wad of paper handkerchiefs that he handed to Raven. The squad car's revolving light was flashing over their heads. The cop nodded across at the *Albatross*. "Do you mind if we look around?"

"Help yourselves," said Raven and led the way.

The two men had their notebooks out as they stepped onto the muddy deck. The fireman peered over the side, staring down at the pieces of rope floating in the slack water below. "You'd have been in big trouble if the fire had really taken ahold."

Raven nodded, aware that he was tired, dirty, and hurting in several places. A strong smell of gasoline lifted on the breeze. Both officers wrinkled their noses. The cop was young and keen. Raven knew the type, eager to demonstrate that he was destined for better things. Blood saturated the tissues Raven was holding against his eyebrow. He threw the soiled pad over the side.

"Know something?" demanded the fireman. "I'd say this thing was started with a can of gasoline and a box of matches." He gouged charred wood with his thumbnail and sniffed at the result. "Sprayed with a watering can. Whoever did it is a dedicated arsonist. Where were you when all this was happening, Mr.—er—Raven?"

Raven found a crumpled pack of cigarettes in his pants. He fished one out and lit it. "I was asleep in my bed, aft on the other side of the boat. I didn't hear a damn thing. The dog barking woke me up."

The light was still going round on the police car. Raven could hear the voices on the radio. The fireman shoved aside a broken flowerpot, using the toe of his gumboot.

"Arson," he repeated. "That's what we're dealing with here. Any idea who might be responsible, any enemies for instance? What line of work are you in?"

The people on the other boats had returned to their beds. There was no sign of Saul Belasus or the Great Dane. Just the crews of the prowl car and the fire engine and the three of them standing down here playing daft games at one-thirty in the morning. Raven picked his words carefully.

"I don't *have* a line of work but I was a cop for seventeen years and that's no grounding for a popularity contest."

The fireman frowned. "You get all sorts, of course. We had a joker last year, a librarian. He set light to twelve churches before they caught up with him."

"Is that so?" said Raven. "Well, there's one thing I suppose I ought to mention. The boat's well-insured and I shall be putting in a substantial claim."

Both men looked slightly embarrassed. The young cop's manner was respectful. "I hope you don't think . . . I mean there's no suggestion that you're personally involved."

"But I *am* involved," Raven said resignedly. "Someone just tried to burn me out and I'd like to go to my bed. What exactly is it that you want from me?"

They exchanged brief glances and the fireman went first. "Nothing much as far as I'm concerned. If you could manage to come to the station sometime tomorrow. I mean today. Ask for me personally—Bill Manners. All I'll want is a simple statement."

The policeman snapped the elastic on his notebook. "I'll make my report but the C.I.D. will probably want to have a word with you."

Raven nodded, yawning. He accompanied them to the bottom of the steps in the Embankment. It was odd stepping back onto the filthy deck with the mud, upturned pots and flowers. He'd have to get hold of some carpenters. The first thing would be to put in a new gangway. All that was left of the old one was one door upright and a tangle of wire. There'd be glass to put in and he'd have to buy new plants and shrubs. Anger built in his mind as he locked and bolted the door from the deck. He showered the dirt and blood from his body. The blankets they had used were on the bathroom floor, scorched beyond further use. He stuck a fresh piece of tape on his eyebrow and sat on the edge of the bed in the darkness. He couldn't see Kirstie's face but he sensed that she was still awake.

"You realize what's happened, don't you?" he asked gently. He answered his own question. "No way could that have been an accident. Some maniac did his level best to burn us out."

Her hand groped for his and held it tightly. "I'm scared, John. *Why* don't we go to the police?"

"That's where I'm heading," he said. "First thing in the morning. But all I'm telling them is what they already know. That some bastard doused us with petrol and put a match to it."

"I'm really sorry I got you into all this," she whispered. "If it hadn't been for me . . ."

"Move over," he ordered. He got into bed and took her in his arms. "Now listen, you want to know who's responsible for your brother's death, right?" He felt her head move in assent. "OK. These bastards know that we're getting close, that we're breathing down their necks. One thing is certain. The fire tonight is linked to the stuff in the envelope we took from the insurance offices. Let's get some sleep."

He opened his eyes on an oblong patch of sunlight slanting across the ceiling. The windows were open and the smell of burned wood hung in the air. Memory soured his initial feeling of well-being. Kirstie's place in the bed was empty. His battered traveling clock showed almost nine o'clock. He had overslept by nearly two hours for the first time in years. Kirstie heard him move and called from the kitchen.

"Stay right where you are! I'm fixing you a tray."

The toweling robe was on the floor where she had dropped it, streaked with dried blood. He pulled it on and padded out to the kitchen. The tray she had prepared was on the table, coffee, grapefruit, and bacon. She was wearing a flowered Camargue shirt, green cotton pants, and matching hair ribbon. She smiled and kissed him, looking as though she hadn't a care in the world. He peered out of the starboard window. The deck outside had been swept and washed, the debris stuffed into plastic disposal sacks. He turned away and sat down at the table.

"Stealing my heart gently," he said. "You didn't have to clear up that mess."

She straddled the chair facing him and leaned her elbows on its back. "Why shouldn't I? It's as much my problem as yours."

He nibbled at a piece of bacon. "I just wish you wouldn't feel so guilty about everything. It's making me edgy."

"I love you, Mr. Raven," she said.

He pushed his plate away suddenly. "I can't eat, Kirstie. I don't have any appetite."

She shrugged and cleared the table. "You ought to eat but what the hell! It's obvious that you've been doing whatever you wanted for years. Why would you change for me?"

He wasn't really listening. "You know what they told me last night? Some cabdriver passing by saw the fire and turned in the alarm. Otherwise we'd have been burned alive. And after all I've said about cabdrivers in the past."

"How about Mrs. Burrows?" she asked.

He hit his forehead with the heel of his hand. "Jesus, God! Would you believe it, I'd completely forgotten about her. She'll have a fit when she arrives. What's the time?" He looked at the kitchen clock.

"I'll be here to break the news," she promised.

He finished his coffee, frowning. "It's what she's been expecting. Her friend with the Tarot cards told her. Disaster on the water and me getting zapped. She'll put it all down to what she refers to as my 'undercover work.' A man comes to the door selling brushes and it's something to do with my undercover work. *You're* probably something to do with my undercover work. She's a born sensationalist. What *do* you propose to tell her?

"The truth," she replied. "It's so much easier. In any case I'm such a lousy liar."

"She's been waiting for something like this to happen for years," he said, shaking his head. "There was some trouble a year or so ago. It involved North Koreans and I was interviewed on television. Mrs. B. saw the program. Since then she won't even buy a Chinese takeaway."

She smiled and he was glad that she was there, the boat gently riding the river, the sunshine streaming in behind her.

"Was last night the end of it, John?" she asked quietly.

The sleeves of the robe flapped as he threw an arm in denial. "More like the beginning. But I'll promise you one thing, my love. Things are going to be a whole lot different from now on. Young Lochinvar is come out of the West. Fuck 'em.'"

"I wish you'd do something about that eye," she said, studying it. "Either leave it alone or go see a doctor and have it stitched."

"There's no time for trivialities," he said, rising. "I'm going to take a bath."

He left the bathroom, put on his blue short-sleeved shirt, jeans, and his Road Runner sneakers and went through to the sitting room. Kirstie was at the desk, writing a letter. He reached over her shoulder and took the insurance company envelope from a drawer.

"I'm going to put this stuff in the bank."

The letter in front of her was in French. "I'm writing to Jacques Bialgues," she explained.

He tucked the envelope in his shirt pocket. "That's nice."

She made a face at him. "There's absolutely no need to be jealous. He's my agent in Paris. He'll be wondering what happened to me."

"And that's nice too," he said. He sat down and lifted the telephone.

She put her letter in its envelope and sealed it carefully. "He's wall-eyed and he chews garlic for a stomach complaint."

"I like him," said Raven, and dialed Jerry Soo's number.

"You've got two minutes," his friend said. "I'm a busy man on his way to the factory."

"I need to see you," said Raven. "Sometime this morning."

"The Greek's at noon," said Soo.

"I'm there." Raven cut the connection.

Kirstie looked at him from the desk. "You didn't say anything about last night."

"That's right," said Raven. "There are things that Jerry prefers not to know and things that he's better off not knowing. Last night happens to fall into both categories."

Her face was suddenly thoughtful. "In any case it would upset Louise and I think she might be pregnant."

He glanced up, put off balance by her suggestion. "How do you know?"

"I don't," she replied. "It's just a feeling that I have."

The fire hadn't touched the interior of the room. The only sign of damage were the cracked windowpanes. Anger rekindled as he thought of the jeopardy his possessions had been put in. The things that he had learned to love over the years, books, paintings, his record collection.

Kirstie loped like a leopard to his side and put her suntanned arms around his neck. Her flesh smelled of the Hermès scent she wore.

"You're scowling. Don't do it!"

"Those bastards," he said with feeling. "With any sort of luck we've got them on the sprint."

She touched his face with her hand. "You're seeing Jerry?"

"As soon as I'm through with the police and the fire brigade."

Her fingers lingered on his cheek before she moved away. "I'm restless. I feel that I ought to be doing more than I am."

"There's plenty for you to do," he replied. "You can get hold of some carpenters for a start. We need a new gangway and there's the glass to replace, tiles. All kinds of things. Mrs. Burrows should be able to help. And listen, same thing as yesterday. If I'm not back here by six o'clock, stay with Saul. I don't care if it's on his boat or in the store but *stay* with him. OK?"

"OK," she promised. "And I want you to take extra special care."

He roped the plank to Saul's boat so that it would be easier for her to cross. Belasus was drinking coffee in his wheelhouse.

"I've told my lady she's to come to you if I'm not back by six," said Raven. "Take care of her. We're having a few problems."

Belasus combed through his beard with his fingers, eyes bright behind his granny glasses.

"I've been getting the vibes. Well, you know me, man. I'm not really into violence but if there's anything I can do . . ."

"Thanks," said Raven.

"Anytime." The herbalist showed his teeth.

The visit to the Fire Brigade occupied ten minutes, no more than a matter of repeating what Raven had said the night before. He drove the half-mile and parked outside Chelsea Police Station. The man in the C.I.D. room seemed to know all about him and treated him with caution. The bare dusty room was furnished with Ministry of Environment desks and chairs. The calendar was supplied by a Birmingham maker of handcuffs. WANTED notices hung on the walls and there was the usual display of chipped, dirty crockery. It was all very familiar and forgettable as far as Raven was concerned. The C.I.D. man was wearing a denim jacket and teeth too perfect to be real.

"That's it then," he said cagily. "But there's not a lot we can do with what you've given us. You realize that?"

"I do," said Raven. "But don't feel too badly about it. I'll try to think of you all as doing your best."

He went downstairs to find a parking ticket attached to his windshield wiper. He dropped it down the nearest drain cover.

Five to twelve. The construction crew from the corner site occupied half the café, with plates of bacon sandwiches and mugs of stewed tea in front of them. The Greek greeted Raven from the kitchen doorway, wiping his forehead with the cloth that was tied around his neck.

"Was good, the meal, yes?"

"Fantastic," said Raven.

The Greek nodded at the far corner. "The Chinaman's there."

Raven pulled the spare chair at Soo's table. His friend was dressed in charcoal-gray flannel and a sober tie.

"Good morning," said Raven. "Where's your *Financial Times*?"

Soo offered his square smile, a ray of sunshine striking through the bristle of black hair to his yellow scalp.

"The nerve center of the Metropolitan Police Force! When you're in a responsible position you have to dress accordingly."

Coke was the safest beverage. The Greek brought Raven a bottle and glass, gave a token flourish at the table with his neck-rag and left. Raven lowered his voice.

"There's a lot happening, Jerry, and I need some information."

Soo switched his toothpick from one side of his mouth to the other. "You're not tripping over your cock, I hope."

Raven reddened. "What exactly is that supposed to mean?"

Soo displayed a palm. "Kirstie. Louise tells me that she's moved in with you."

Raven took a deep breath. "That's right. She has moved

in with me and I want her to stay. I don't know if that answers your question?"

His friend's grin expanded. "No, but the look on your face does. She's a nice girl, John."

"I know that," answered Raven. "You told me so at the beginning when I came to your flat."

They eyed one another warily then Soo gave a formal little bow like an exponent of the martial arts acknowledging his adversary.

"What's your problem, John?"

Raven searched the boot-button eyes. Certain types of news traveled very quickly over the police network. He was fairly certain that the attempt to fire the boat would be known at the Yard. Calls would be made, winks of congratulation exchanged. He decided that Jerry could find out for himself.

"Is Denton bent?" Raven demanded.

"In what sense do you mean?"

Raven leaned forward confidentially. "I told you that things are happening. I'm beginning to get a picture that makes me think Kirstie is right. I think that they set her brother up for the reward. I've read the transcript of his trial and I don't see how the villainy could have been done unless Denton was in on it."

Soo put his toothpick away. "Denton is a first-class bastard and I don't think he has all his marbles but he's cunning, ambitious, and smart. He wouldn't touch a penny of crooked money."

Raven nodded slowly. "I'll accept that but he's got to be in there somewhere. Just take a look at these." He passed the envelope across the table.

Soo opened the envelope and examined the contents, holding each item close to his chest.

"Where did you get this stuff?"

"I didn't hear you," Raven said, shaking his head. "You

must know the way these things are done, Jerry. The insurance companies require an official letter from the police
identifying the claimant as the man entitled to the reward.
The letter always goes out over the Commissioner's signature but it's the officer in charge of the case who supplies
the details. That means that Denton vouched for this
George Smith and knows his real identity."

Soo's gold tooth showed. "So?"

"I haven't checked the address on that receipt but you
can lay odds it's a phony. And look at those photographs.
What I'm saying is that George Smith is Denton's nark and
not some sharp-eyed member of the public."

"Where's your proof of that?"

Raven lifted a shoulder. "OK, I don't *have* any proof. All
I have is a gut feeling and seventeen years' experience. Can
you get into Criminal Records without alarms going off all
over the place?"

"Yes."

"Then I want those prints checked, Jerry. As soon as you
can. It's very important.

Soo tucked the envelope in an inside pocket. "Have you
been running into another doorway?" he asked, looking at
Raven's eyebrow.

Raven touched the tape self-consciously. "How soon can
you get back to me, Jerry?"

Soo consulted his nickel-plated pocket watch. "An
hour? Maybe less. It all depends on whether my man is on
duty."

"About Kirstie," Raven said suddenly. "I'm not playing
games."

"I'm glad to hear it." Jerry Soo's face was unexpectedly
serious. "She isn't either. I hope it works. You've both got
as much chance as anyone else."

Raven gave it a few minutes, tipped his chair to reserve
his seat, and went out to buy a copy of the midday *Standard*.

He took it back to the café and read it thoroughly, deaf to
the noise around him. There was no mention of the fire in
the newspaper. He looked up as the door opened. It was
twenty to one by the clock above the kitchen door. Jerry
Soo's face was difficult to read. He placed the envelope on
the table in front of Raven.

"Clean," he announced. "No record."

The words dropped like stones in Raven's head. The
picture he had painted in his mind depended on the owner
of the fingerprints having a police record.

"Fuck it," he said frustratedly.

Soo grinned and produced a sheet of paper, lapsing into
chop suey English. "Chinahboy velly clevah!" He pushed
the sheet of paper at Raven. "Read it," he said in his normal voice.

What he had in his hands was a photocopy of an application for a South American visa, dated the previous year
and written on a consular form. There was space on the
form for certification that the applicant had no criminal
record.

NAME John Jubal
DATE & PLACE OF BIRTH London, February 2 1942
NATIONALITY British
PASSPORT NUMBER C21964
OCCUPATION Company director
ADDRESS Godhawk Timber & Sawmills Lost Lane W. 12

The top left-hand corner bore the official stamp of the
Metropolitan Police. Lower down was the rubber imprint
of a travel agency.

"It comes from the Dirty Tricks Department," said Soo,
"and I've got to get it back there right away."

Raven shook his head. "I don't get it."

"There's no big deal," said Soo. "The iron brain rejected

the prints the first time round. No criminal record. Then my man had a brain wave, a rush of genius to the head. He asked another question. You're looking at the result. The thing is, C.R.O. has had a file on Jubal for years as a known associate of villains. So when the travel agency sent in the visa application for processing, some bright bastard photocopied it."

Raven scribbled the details in his little book. "There was no mention of Denton anywhere?"

"Not a thing," said Soo. "Here's Denton's home number. It might be useful."

Raven returned the photocopy.

"You're not just devious, you're brilliant."

Soo came to his feet again, his face serious. "Don't get out of your depth, John. Holler for help if you need it."

Raven looked up, smiling. "You're forgetting something. As I recall it was you who came to me for help. I'll be in touch."

The Greek took Raven's money. "Food good, lady good, ha?" He slapped his right biceps with the palm of his left hand and shot the arm out. A couple of the construction workers hooted.

Raven thought of adopting an air of refined distaste but decided it would be a waste of time. "Watch your mouth," he said instead. "Or you might have problems."

The Greek was aware of dramatic possibilities and struck himself hard on the chest. "Probbles? Every fuckin' day I got probbles! I got probbles from my old wooman and Health Inspector, I got probbles from little kids onna street and my friend want to give me more probbles!" He grinned and repeated the obscene gesture he had made before.

Raven closed the door on the Greek's bubbling laughter. He drove to the bank on Knightsbridge Green. He had a small account there, an excuse to rent a safety-deposit box he had held for nine years. He signed the book and used his key, together with the bank official. Inside the box were his birth certificate, a bundle of his mother's love letters and some snapshots of her, five thousand illegally held Swiss francs, and some poetry he had written while at Harrow. He sealed the insurance company folder in an envelope, wrote the date on the front, and locked it up in the vault.

Half an hour later he was in the wastes beyond Shepherd's Bush. The Godhawk Timber Yard and Sawmill was at the far end of an approach road that was bordered by heavy-gauge wire fencing. He left the Citroën near a pair of back-to-back telephone booths and strolled to the other end of the approach road. Beyond the sturdy wire fence was a no man's land of rusting car bodies, decay of all kinds, stagnant water, and flowering weeds. Tall wooden gates sealed the end of the road. There was a buzzer and a speaking tube by the side of a wicket door. The sign above it read OFFICE. He put his eye to the crack and saw a small office building, drying sheds for green timber and a sawmill. He could hear the high-pitched whine of steel teeth ripping through logs. Men were loading planks onto a five-ton truck.

He walked back as far as the phone booths. There was a bus stop not far away but the street was deserted, hot under the sun and flanked on both sides by desolation. The only sign of movement in fifty acres came from the timber yard. Raven opened the door of the nearest phone booth, found the number of the timber yard, and dialed. The call was promptly answered by a girl's voice.

"Godhawk Timber. Good morning, may I help you?"

"I'd like to speak to Mr. Jubal," said Raven.

"Hold the line," she said. "I'll see if he's available. May I have your name, please."

"Smith," he said. "George Smith."

It was hot in the booth. He stuck a foot in the door and held it open. A breath of air carried a reek that smelled as though it emanated from a glue factory. The girl's voice came on again.

"I'm afraid Mr. Jubal isn't in today. Would you like to leave a message?"

He held the phone between chin and shoulder and lit the cigarette in his mouth. "Then maybe you could give me Mr. Jubal's home number. I have it at home but not with me."

"We're not allowed to do that," she said. "Strict orders from Mr. Jubal himself."

He blew smoke through the open doorway. "I don't think you understand," said Raven. "This isn't only a personal matter, it's urgent."

"I'm sorry, sir," she started, and changed her mind. "I'm putting you through to the manager."

She clicked him over to the sound of a man's voice. "Can I be of any help, sir?"

Raven repeated what he had said to the girl. The man wasted no time. "The best I can do for you is to take your number, sir, and have Mr. Jubal call you back. What did you say your name was?"

"George Smith," said Raven, and gave him the number of the phone booth. "Is Mr. Jubal at home, do you know?"

"I talked to him just five minutes ago. Hang up and I'll tell him that you're waiting."

Raven replaced the receiver and stationed himself outside the door. A woman had appeared about a hundred yards away and was coming toward him, heading for the bus stop or the phone. He needed both booths if his plan was to work. She was only fifty yards away when the phone rang behind him. Raven reached in and lifted the receiver.

The Cockney voice was low and wary. "Mr. Smith?"

"One moment, please," said Raven. "I'll get him for

you." He left the phone on top of the coin box, rushed into the next door booth and called the Postal Engineers Department.

"This is Detective-Sergeant Venables, Scotland Yard." Raven gave the police code for service and the number of the other booth. "Somebody's on this line. I want the call traced and the name and address of the subscriber. And hurry!"

The woman had halted at the bus stop, putting her shopping basket on the ground, grateful for the shelter from the sun. Seconds stretched into a minute. Raven's eyes were on the phone in the neighboring booth, willing Jubal to stay on the line. The engineer came back.

"The name is John Jubal, nine four three–zero zero eight three, ex-directory. The address is twenty-four Parkway, Richmond."

Raven hung up, moved next door, and replaced the receiver. The woman at the bus-stop shelter watched him curiously as he opened the Citroën and took the wheel. Jubal's address was on a road facing Richmond Park. Beyond a wooden palisade, children were cantering ponies along an avenue of burgeoning beech trees. Water sparkled in the distance. This was no longer the endless rows of Victorian villas, the back yards with flapping wet wash on the drying lines. This was broad tree-lined avenues with detached houses made private with hedges and walls. Raven knew the neighborhood to be popular with people in the entertainment industry. The local residents' association had successfully resisted a government attempt to take over part of the park.

Number twenty-four was a red-brick house with white-painted windows and gates at the ends of a hooped driveway. The front windows and garage were open. Raven climbed three steps and pressed a button. He heard a bell ring inside but nobody answered. He tried again with no more success. He walked across the asphalt driveway. It was a three-car garage but the only vehicle there was a green Volkswagen. Raven crossed the oil-stained concrete to the back of the garage and turned a door handle. There was just enough time for him to take in trees, a lawn under sunshine, toys scattered over the grass, and a one-eyed Doberman rising on a knoll beneath a chestnut tree. Then things happened rapidly. The Doberman launched itself, flat-eared, lips drawn back from savage-looking fangs.

Seventeen-year-old instructions flashed through Raven's mind, the training sergeant in charge of police dogs and their handlers, his nose cherry-red from gin and the cold.

"There is," he would bawl, "'owever, one infallerbil method of meeting a 'ostile animal's charge. By fust protecting the juggler vein with a length of 'andy material and dropping on one knee *so!*" Here he had illustrated the movement stiffly. "Avoiding the brute's ravernous jaws, you seize its front legs and wrench them apart *so!* Thus busting the fucker's chest cavity!"

Raven barely managed to close the garage door on the Doberman. The framework rattled as the animal thudded against the planks. The dog was silent but he knew that it was still there. He retreated from the garage. The front door of the house opened as he backed onto the driveway. The woman standing there was in her early thirties, her white dress showing off her suntan. Her mascara had run. She watched narrowly as Raven came toward her. He stopped at the foot of the steps.

"Good afternoon. Is Mr. Jubal at home?"

She was wearing a diamond solitaire and wedding ring on the same finger. Her speech was somewhat slurred.

"No, he's not. What do you want him for?"

"It's a personal matter." He smiled to take the edge off the phrase.

She inspected him thoroughly and looked across at the Citroën. "Is that your car?"

He nodded, maintaining his affability. "You're quite sure that he isn't in?"

"My husband isn't here," she said, reaching down as the Doberman tried to pass her. She caught the animal by its steel mesh collar. The Doberman was whining, its good eye glaring balefully at Raven.

"Perhaps you could tell me when he'll be back?" Raven inquired politely.

"For all I know, never," she said bitterly.

Raven realized that she was slightly drunk. He cleared his throat. "It would be in his own interests if you could help me to get hold of him, Mrs. Jubal."

Her self-control snapped and her voice rose. "I don't know who you are or why you're here. But I can tell you this much, if you're not off this property in ten seconds I'm turning the dog loose."

Raven gauged the distance to the car. The Doberman could give him twenty yards' start and still catch him. He forced himself to saunter towards the Citroën, his buttocks and the backs of his legs feeling very vulnerable. He glanced across at the house from the driver's seat but the front door was closed. He stopped at the first call-box he saw and telephoned the houseboat. Mrs. Burrows answered, her voice edged with indignation.

"A nice thing for me to see first thing in the morning, I must say! It gave me a fair turn."

"Is Miss Macfarlane there?" asked Raven.

"No, she is not. I wonder you don't give it up, Mr. Raven."

"Give what up?" he asked patiently.

She clucked disapproval. "You know perfectly well what I'm talking about. The secret service is what! And you with

a nice lady like her in your life. You ought to start thinking
about your responsibilities."

He lost his patience suddenly. "Worry about the dust
under my bed, Mrs. Burrows. I'll take care of my responsibilities. Do you happen to know where Miss Macfarlane has
gone?"

Mrs. Burrows sounded somewhat shaken by his outburst. "I sent her to Blackstone's, the builders, near where
I live. She said you wanted carpenters. And by the way, you
didn't leave no shopping list today."

It wasn't easy to put her in her place but he made the
effort. "Miss Macfarlane will be attending to that."

There was a short silence before she sniffed. "Then I'd
better get on with the ironing. I don't suppose she'll be
attending to *that*, will she?"

"Thank you, Mrs. Burrows," he said. "And don't forget
the dust under the beds." He put the phone down quickly.

The Herborium was closed when he reached the Embankment. He backed into the alleyway. The curtains of
Saul's store were at their usual half-mast. A live gecko,
poised as still as stone, eyed him from the window. He
ducked through the traffic to the river and ran down the
steps. There was no door to Saul's gangway. Low tide gave
his neighbor's boat an exaggerated tilt. The Great Dane
bounded to meet him. He fended it off and found Kirstie
and the Californian sitting in the sun on the other side of
the wheelhouse. Raven kissed the back of Kirstie's neck,
shaking his head at Saul's offer of a beer.

"I won't, thanks. There's a lot to be done."

Kirstie stretched and yawned, catlike for a moment as
she screwed up her eyes. She opened them again and
smiled.

"There's quite a lot that has been done. Mrs. Burrows
sent me to some people she knows. The man was here this
afternoon, looking at the damage. He's going to call to-

morrow morning with an estimate. If that's OK with you he can start work immediately. He said that he ought to be through in four or five days. They'll make the gangway in their workshop and assemble it here."

The smile she was giving him was as physical as though her hand had touched his. The Great Dane laid the weight of its massive head on Raven's knee, its gentle strength in contrast to the savagery of the Doberman.

"No calls?" asked Raven. "No messages?"

"Lassiter," she said meaningfully, and left it at that.

"Right," Raven said, standing. "Thanks for looking after her, Saul."

The Californian's beard wagged. "You know me, John. The original stand-up guy. Any time at all, Kirstie. It'll be a real pleasure."

Raven handed Kirstie across the plank to the *Albatross*. The deck had been thoroughly cleaned. Kirstie used her keys to let them into the sitting room. He was conscious of subtle changes. Chairs had been moved around. Red carnations blazed on his desk.

"Lassiter," he reminded.

She picked up the telephone pad. "He called just before lunch and asked for you. He didn't seem at all surprised that it was I who answered."

He opened a drawer in his desk and took out the thirty-eight.

"What did Lassiter want?"

"To talk to you. He left this number." She gave him the pad.

He sat down near the phone, the pad on his knee, and explained. "Jerry ran a check on those prints. They belong to someone called Jubal. He doesn't have a police record himself but he's a known associate of people who do. I managed to track him down finally."

She listened, a shoe dangling from her bare foot as she

jiggled her leg. She glanced across at the gun on top of the desk. "What do you propose to do with that?"

"I don't know that I like the sound of that question," he replied. "I hope you're not going to disappoint me."

She looked at him coolly. "You mean you're disappointed because I'm concerned about you?"

He shrugged. "How can I win? What I'm trying to say is this. We're getting very close to the people who framed your brother. We know at least one of them and we know why he did it. This is no time to get squeamish."

She uncrossed her legs. "It isn't a matter of getting squeamish, John, Quite simply, I'm worried about you getting hurt. Surely we've got enough to go to the police with?"

"Not a chance," he answered. "Don't forget I was a cop for seventeen years and I know how they think. OK, I might be able to get in to see an Assistant Commissioner. What do I tell him? That I burgled the insurance offices and stole a file with Jubal's fingerprints and pictures? Jubal is a police-informer and that's a protected species. Don't you see, darling. There's nothing yet that *can* be proven."

She pushed her hair back with a quick nervous gesture. "It's the gun that worries me."

"It worries me too," he said. "But I'd sooner have it and be worried than the other way around. We're dealing with violent men. I've been beaten up and had my home set alight. I'm not taking any chances with Jubal."

She let her breath go and stood up. "What exactly are you going to do about him?"

"Pay him another visit. I'm going back tonight. And if I don't find him then, then tomorrow. And the next day and so on till I *do* find him."

Her smile was rueful. "I never realized what I was getting into with you. Don't you ever give up?"

"Rarely," he said. "What you have to understand, my

sweet, is that this has become a very personal thing for me. It isn't just Jamie anymore."

"And you're going there tonight?"

He nodded his head. "As soon as it's dark."

"Then I'm coming with you," she said firmly.

It was what he had expected her to say and he gave her no argument. "Fair enough," he replied. "We've done everything else together, why not this?"

She came close enough for him to touch the pulse beating on her neck. "It *is* real, isn't it, John?" she demanded. "I mean between us?"

"It's real," he promised, and put his mouth on hers.

She broke away and went into the bathroom. Raven dialed the number that Lassiter had left. The lawyer answered.

"Look, this may not be of much importance but Denton called me this morning. The excuse was to know if Kirstie had received her brother's effects safely. What he really wanted to know was about you. I told him nothing, of course."

"Thanks," said Raven. "And thanks for letting me know."

"How's it coming along?" In spite of what he had previously said about not wanting to be involved, Lassiter's voice was oddly curious.

Raven hesitated, uncertain whether or not to take the lawyer into his confidence. He decided to go halfway. "I'd like to ask you a question. If I come to you with proof that Jamie was framed, will you act?"

"Act for whom?"

"I don't know for whom." Raven found the niceties of legal jargon intensely irritating. "But *act!* Help clear Macfarlane's name."

"Get the proof and we'll talk about it," said Lassiter. "And watch your step."

Raven went through to the bedroom. Kirstie had slipped off her shoes and was lying on the bed with her hands behind her head.

"What are you thinking about?" he challenged.

She turned her head sideways. "You and me. That love should never be analyzed but just accepted. I'll have to go to Paris soon."

He felt a twinge of jealous despair. "What for?"

"Both of us," she said. "I want you to see my apartment. I'm going to have to make plans. Did I tell you that Louise called?"

He sat down on the side of the bed, his hand on the warm flesh of her upper thigh. "And?"

She stirred slightly under his touch. "Not very much. What she was trying to say was that no matter what, you would enrich my life. A poetic way of putting it. I told her that I already knew that."

9. Smiling Jack Jubal

HE KNEW that it was late when he woke. Sunlight pierced the chink in the curtains and shone on the empty whisky glass by his bedside. The house was unusually quiet, which meant that he was the only one in it. The girl would have taken the twins to school and Millie must have left for work. He padded to the bathroom in his underpants, gargled, and splashed his face with cold water. There was no gray in his straw-colored hair. His teeth were his own, and he had held the same weight for the past eleven years. Not too bad for thirty-six. He slipped on a robe, went downstairs, and collected the mail and newspapers from the table in the hallway. The dog was probably outside somewhere. He went through to the kitchen. The toast in the rack was stone cold, the tea in the pot barely warm. He'd spent nearly four grand equipping the kitchen alone, everything of the best and bought at last year's Ideal Home Exhibition. Deep-freeze, infrared stove, a washing machine as big as Millie's Volkswagen, and a brand new Grundig color television. There must have been half a ton of pure aluminum in the place, he thought, looking round disgustedly. And the bitch couldn't even leave him a decent breakfast.

He poured the lukewarm tea and buttered stale toast, too lazy to prepare fresh. He could see the Doberman, its head on its paws, asleep under the tree. The gardener was up by the pool, doing something with a pair of shears. Another lazy bugger, who spent most of his time messing around in the garage. Jubal leafed through the mail. There was nothing of interest. He put his plate and cup on the drainboard and spread the first newspaper out on the table. He took the *Sun* for sport, the *Mail* and *Express* for gossip—you sometimes picked up useful bits of information—and the *Telegraph* for the court reports. He went through all four papers very carefully without finding any mention of a fire in Chelsea Reach. It might have been too late to make these editions. He lit the first cheroot of the day, leaned back and closed his eyes. His wife's voice disturbed his reverie. He opened one eye at a time.

Millie was standing in the hallway door, her hands on her hips. Like the shrew she was, he thought sourly.

"It's about time you and me came to a proper sort of understanding," she said. "I'm not going to go on being treated like a piece of dirt. I'm your wife."

He removed the cheroot from his mouth very deliberately. Almost everything about her irritated him. The way she looked, the way she dressed, and especially the sound of her voice.

"I don't need reminding who you are," he replied.

The look in her eyes and the set of her mouth made it plain that this was going to be no brief exchange. She took her hands off her hips and sauntered forward into the kitchen.

"You can do whatever you like when you're out of the house," she said. "I couldn't care less about your antics or about all those cheap little whores who take your money and laugh at you behind your back. The girls in the shop do. Laugh at you, I mean. The great lover, hah! But this is my home and it's different. And in front of the kids is different. I want the same thing you're always banging on about. Respect!"

He shifted a piece of burned toast from the back of a molar. "You must be joking, respect! Respect for *what*? You can't even see that I get a proper breakfast."

"You'd get it if you were up," she replied. "I mean what I say, you know."

She was standing with her back to the strong sunlight and he could see the outline of the girdle she had started to wear. "Finished?" he asked sarcastically.

She shut the hallway door, though as far as he could see they were alone in the house. He heard the milkman's van out front.

"No, I have *not* finished," she said.

He was up in a flash. Anger ran with inventiveness and he knew that it was time to act.

"Well, I'll finish for you," he said savagely. "You and me are through, mate. It's all over as of bleedin' *now!* You want money, you can have it, but you'll get it the proper way, through my mouthpiece. And there'll be rules and regulations about what you can do. This place will go on the market and I'll get myself a flat."

Her face looked genuinely shocked. "You mean you're going to leave me! And what about the kids?"

"A *bachelor* flat," he said. "No room for kids. You can get yourself something close to work and spend more time chatting up all them fag hairdressing friends of yours."

"I'd be careful what you say, if I was you. I know a lot more than you think, John Jubal."

He stepped forward and swung hard with his right hand, catching her on the side of her face with his palm. She lifted her hand to her cheek and looked at it as though expecting to see blood.

"That's the last time you ever do that," she said quietly. "I used to love you but I'm learning to hate."

"Piss off to work," he said contemptuously. "You're getting on my tits!"

Her eyes searched his face as if committing it to memory. She left the room, closing the door behind her very carefully. He stuck his head into the drawing room on the way upstairs. She wasn't there but wherever she'd gone she'd taken the fresh bottle of gin with her. Just as long as she got the message. He took his time about dressing, pleased with the turn of events. His hand had been forced in a way, but that didn't matter. He had said all that had to be said. Sometimes things happened this way. Your whole life could change in just a few hours. Millie wasn't a bad girl at heart, a good mother and, as she'd said, loyal enough. The trouble was that they had been too long together, ever since she'd first left school, an apprentice at Dudes and Dandies, the first trendy hairdresser's establishment on King's Road.

He smoothed his hair down over his ears, whistling as he looked into the mirror. His flowered shirt was embroidered with the initials J.J. on the pocket. The nuns did a good job with a needle. His slacks and white loafers were Italian. He made his way down the staircase, still whistling softly. He unlocked his listening post in the library and checked the house for any sign of movement. The girl wasn't back yet and there was no sound from Millie's room. He let himself out through the front door and reversed the Jaguar.

He passed the Swedish *au pair* on her way back from the school, suntanned and graceful. He touched the horn-ring and she waved. There was no harm in trying to give her one now. She'd be going in any case. He was at Hammersmith Broadway when the notion took him. He cut back through Fulham and Chelsea and turned toward the river. Gulls wheeled over the sunlit water. Beyond the bridge was the rich green of Battersea Park. A U-turn into the westbound traffic brought him close to the pavement and the boats on the other side of the retaining wall. He slowed to a crawl, indicator flashing as he neared the small flotilla of houseboats. The picture at the back of his mind had been of a burned-out hull, of twisted strips of metal, evidence of death and total destruction. What he saw unnerved him. He stopped a few hundred yards on, walked back a piece, and leaned over the stone parapet. His first impression had been accurate. Raven's boat was still afloat. The gangway and door at the end had disappeared. The starboard deck and superstructure were charred in places and the flowers and shrubs were gone. He could see people moving on the boat even as he looked, a middle-aged woman with whitish hair hanging something on a line strung across the stern and, incredibly, Kirstie Macfarlane. She was watching the gulls riding the currents of air high overhead. Without a care in the world, he thought bitterly.

He turned away quickly, a sour taste in his mouth. Nothing made sense anymore. All the rules said the *Albatross* should have been burned to a cinder. There'd been gasoline enough. Speculation was useless. The fact was that he had blown it again. This fucker Raven bore a charmed life.

Jubal drove west. Part of his brain handled the controls, the rest was busy assessing the implications of Raven's escape. Because of the failure of his plan, what had seemed so simple the night before began to take on sinister aspects. Phrases like *attempted murder and arson* whispered through his head. He thought of trying to involve Denton in some way but decided against it. His best bet was to keep a very low profile and if the worst came to tough it out. In any case they had no proof. No one had seen him near Raven's boat. There was nothing to connect him with fire-setting. Uneasiness lingered in spite of his attempts at self-reassurance. By the time he arrived at the timber yard, uneasiness had changed to apprehension. He left the Jaguar outside his office and used his private entrance. The clothes he had worn the previous night still stank of gasoline. There was no longer any question of having them dry-cleaned. He put them in a plastic bag, walked out into the sunshine, and made his way to the rear of one of the seasoning sheds. He put a match to the clothing, watching until it had burned completely. He dispersed the charred remnants with his foot and returned to his office. He used the phone, feeling a whole lot better. He had brief words with his lawyer and made an appointment to discuss Millie and the future. It came as a shock to him to hear his lawyer talking in terms of divorce. This wasn't what Jubal really had in mind. A legal separation was more like it, with Millie at far remove but still under some sort of control.

He opened the outside door and sat in the sun doing his sums. The salon was in Millie's name though he had bought it. The business should give her a fair living. He'd throw in another couple of grand and something in trust for the twins. He chewed the end of the felt pen, looking down at his figures. He could never abandon England permanently but there was no reason why he shouldn't take a trip abroad again. South America, for instance. His visas were still current and he'd enjoy himself better this time without Millie banging on about everything—the people, the food and the water. That was it, put the house up for sale and take a long holiday. By the time he came back, Millie would be installed somewhere else and the Macfarlane business would be forgotten.

He burned the slip of paper with his sums in the ashtray. Strange how easy it was to try to kill someone and have no feelings about it. His one concern was self-preservation. And why not? People talked a lot of bullshit about why they did this and that but the truth was simple. Everything you did of any importance was based on the will to survive. Otherwise you were a loser. He locked his office and drove to a nearby diner. In spite of his taste for better things, he was happy eating in the company of people like this.

Truckdrivers, workers from the nearby building site, people who recognized him as one of their own who had made it. He ordered bacon, sausages, and eggs, and a glass of cold milk. He paid his bill and returned to the Jaguar. Millie would be out of the house by now and he needed to get into her bedroom. The safe was there and there was something in it that had to be removed without her breathing down his neck.

Millie's Volkswagen was still in the garage. He drove in and opened the garden door. The *au pair* was by the pool, sitting on the end of the diving board, reading, a handkerchief tied round her head. She was wearing only the bottom half of her bikini. Her breasts were brown and bare. The one-eyed Doberman came to greet Jubal, growling softly and semaphoring with its stump-tail. Jubal went in through the kitchen. Someone had eaten. The remains of a meal were on the table. The telephone rang as he crossed the hallway. He took the call in his study. It was the works manager with an inquiry about a customer's credit. Jubal put him right and made his way upstairs. Millie's bedroom was ajar. She was lying on her back on the bed, fully dressed with her eyes closed and one arm trailing. His first thought was that she had killed herself. Closer inspection showed that she was breathing. Her mouth was open and her hair snarled. There were four empty tonic water bottles on the bedside table and half the gin had gone. The safe was behind a picture over the bed. There was no chance of opening it without waking her.

He crossed the landing to his own room and picked up the phone on the first ring. It was the yard manager again.

"A man has been calling you here. He says it's important and urgent and he's left a number for you to call back."

Jubal dragged his eyebrows together in a frown. "Did he give a name?"

"Yes, he did. George Smith."

Jubal felt as though his blood had stopped running. He heard himself speak with a total sense of unreality.

"Give me the number."

He hung up quickly, closed the bedroom door, and dialed. An unknown voice answered.

"Mr. Smith?" Jubal asked guardedly.

"One moment, I'll get him for you."

It was difficult to identify the background noises at the other end of the line. A restaurant or club, possibly. Jubal waited anxiously. Suddenly the line went dead. His caller had hung up on him. Jubal's movements were instinctive. He ran downstairs, jumped into the Jaguar, and gunned it out to the street. For the moment he had no idea where he was going, his only thought to put distance between him and danger. He drove aimlessly through the park and onto the Guildford road. Fifteen miles south, he pulled the Jaguar off the highway onto a lane overhung with foliage and dappled with sunshine. He followed it to the end, a clearing by a river in the heart of the beech wood. A disused mill stood above a dark race of weir water, its paddles permanently poised. He left the car and sat with his legs dangling over the sluice gate.

George Smith *had* to be Raven. But how had he made the connection with Jubal? It wouldn't be through Denton. It was in Denton's interests to stand well clear and he made a point of establishing this. A fish swirled suddenly, breaking the surface of the water in quest of an insect. Trees crowded in on both sides of the river, alders and willows leaning from the grassy banks. The stillness was complete, broken only by the occasional cry of a crow. Jubal walked back to the mill. The timber was bleached and weathered. The windows had long since been broken. A safe place to hide was what he needed, he thought. Well, not so much hide as disappear. Back in the car, he made his decision.

He was going to need cash. Only a mug risked carrying sterling through customs these days. Penalties were severe for offenses against the Exchange Control Act. It was safer to pay 4 or 5 percent brokerage to one of the Hatton Garden specialists and pick up your money at your destination, Swiss francs or D marks. Dollars were chancy at the moment, up and down like a yo-yo.

He drove back to London. By six o'clock he had completed his travel arrangements. He had a flight ticket to Caracas at twenty hours forty on the following day and a letter to a Señor Valdes of the same city. The letter guaranteed a payment of fifteen thousand Swiss francs, ample for the time he expected to stay in Venezuela. Pleasure and relief grew with each step he took. He was sure that his plan was right, that he was doing the correct thing. He had told people at the yard that he was going abroad on business. To Sweden, he'd said, about as far as he could get from the truth. The yard and sawmills were run on simple lines. There was a backlog of orders and as long as production was steady there could be no problems. Any one of the girls in the office could have run the place. He passed the next few hours in his usual haunts, displaying his usual joviality and taking soundings. There were no strange looks. No ominous silences greeted his arrival. None of the current gossip touched on anything or anyone connected to him. He left the Tabriz Casino at quarter past nine, smoking a ten-inch cigar, the gift of the proprietor. The streetlamps were already on in Richmond Park, the shadows velvet. He turned the Jaguar through the white-painted gates onto the hardtop. Every light in the fucking house seemed to be on. He climbed the steps, hardening his heart and face. Millie was waiting for him, sitting on the bottom rung of the staircase. Her mascara was streaked and her nose was red. She had made no attempt to tidy her hair. Quite plainly she had been drinking again.

"Welcome home!" she said, and smiled lopsidedly. "Lover!"

He stepped past her and went up the stairs. He headed for her bedroom, the key to the safe in his hand. The bed was rumpled, the pillowcase was stained with mascara. The gin bottle was almost empty. His passport was on the safe's bottom shelf. He slipped it into his pocket with the letter to Valdes and his flight ticket. Millie was sitting in the same position when he went downstairs again.

"Where are the kids?" he demanded.

She looked up with eyes that no longer focused properly. "Why don't you go up and see? They're in their beds."

He made no secret of his disgust. "You going to sit there all night? You mean the kids saw you like this?"

She pulled herself up, clutching at the banister rail. "I'm their mother. They know that I love them."

Maudlin, he thought and his eye sharpened to caution. It was neither the time nor the place to spend another night with her. There was no sense in telling her that he had taken advice from Rifkind and was seeing the lawyer the following day. She was too drunk to understand or remember.

"Get a hold on yourself," he advised. "Get some coffee inside you and go up to bed."

"To bed?" She smiled uncertainly.

He was halfway across the hall when the door to the kitchen was opened. The tall thin man standing there was holding a short-barreled pistol in his right hand. He was wearing jeans and sneakers and his eyes were steady.

"Up against the wall!" he ordered. "Hands on top of your head!"

Jubal stepped back carefully. The intruder was the same man who'd been sun-bathing on the deck of the *Albatross*. But where the hell was the dog?

Raven pushed fingers through gray-blond hair, grinning as though he had read Jubal's thoughts. "Pig's liver. Half-cooked. It'll stop anything that ever barked. Empty your pockets onto the table. Everything nice and easy, now."

Jubal tried to moisten his lips and failed. "What do you think you're doing? Who are you?"

Raven's grin widened, acknowledging Millie's presence for the first time. "The man has me beaten up and tried to murder me. Then he wants to know who I am!"

Millie swayed on the bottom step, concentrating hard as she looked from her husband to Raven and back. A television program was tuned in somewhere upstairs.

"What's that?" Raven asked sharply.

Millie hiccupped. "It's the girl. The *au pair!*" She flung an arm in the general direction of the bedrooms.

Jubal gauged the distance to the front door and decided against taking the chance. "If you're not out of here soon, I'm going to call the law."

Raven cocked his head. "That makes a difference, at least. Your wife was going to turn the dog on me."

"You mean he's been here before?" Jubal looked at Millie.

"Shut up!" said Raven. He closed the kitchen door and walked forward. The patch on his left eyebrow added a touch of menace. "You don't say another word unless you're told. Empty your pockets!"

Jubal obeyed, laying one thing after another on the hall table. Money, keys, cheroots. Passport, flight ticket, and the letter to Señor Valdes. He felt as though he had just been asked to take off his clothes and was standing there naked. His hands had started to shake.

Raven flicked through the pages of the passport and air ticket. He stuffed them in his hip pocket and perused the letter. This he added to the other things in his pocket.

"Well, well," he remarked conversationally. "Breaking the currency regulations. Venezuela, no less. How long do you plan to be gone?"

Jubal put his hands back on top of his head. This whole thing was outrageous. The kids and the girl upstairs; this fucker who should have been dead, standing here with a pistol; Millie drunk and his whole life slipping away. Millie suspended her giggling and pointed a wavering hand at Raven.

"I don't know who you are, Mister. And I don't know that I care. But there's something about my husband that you don't know."

Jubal knew what was coming instinctively. There was liquid in his mouth but it was bile and not saliva. Millie smiled at him happily.

"You want to know how he makes a living? He's a fucking grass, that's what! A police-informer. That's right, Smiling Jack Jubal, everyone's stand-up friend! A stinking rotten police-informer!"

Raven's voice was not unkind. "Why don't you go up to bed. Don't worry about your husband. He's going to be just fine, aren't you, Smiler?"

Jubal said nothing. The grandfather clock chimed sonorously, a length of chain rattling somewhere in the case.

Millie dragged herself upright with difficulty. "Little rest," she announced. "Long day. Ask him where he was last night," she said to Raven.

Raven nodded. "We know where he was."

Millie swung her right arm before anyone could prevent her, catching Jubal across the mouth. "For this morning," she said with an attempt at dignity and climbed the stairs slowly, clutching at the banister rail.

"Right," said Raven. He opened the door to the study, snapped the lights off, and prodded Jubal into the dark-

ened room. Jubal heard the curtains run, then the lights
came on again. "Sit!" said Raven.

Jubal put both feet flat on the floor for support. His
mind was jinking like a fox that has broken cover but no
matter which way it ran Raven's face was waiting.

Raven straddled a chair, his forearms on the backrest.
"So you set them up, turn them, and then claim the insurance reward." He shook his head sadly. "You're a real
all-rounder, aren't you?"

Jubal cleared his throat cautiously. The bleedin' dog was
whining out in the garden somewhere, stuffed full of pig's
liver.

"What do you want from me, Raven?" asked Jubal.

"Then you *do* know who I am," Raven said apprecia-
tively.

Jubal offered what he hoped was an open and honest
look. "It's not the way you think. It's not like that at all."

"Then tell me how it is," suggested Raven. He lit a smoke
and offered the pack to Jubal. "Take your time and start at
the beginning."

Jubal took a long drag on the cigarette. The man was
playing games with him. "What is it you want from me?"

"The truth," said Raven. He rested his chin on the back
of his free hand. "Just how you set Macfarlane up. What
Denton got out of it. Why you tried to kill me."

Jubal called on years of subterfuge. "You know your
problem? I'll tell you what your problem is. You've got no
proof of nothing!"

"Wrong," said Raven laconically. "I've got enough to get
you at least indicted."

"I don't believe you," Jubal said stoutly, then wavered.
"For what?"

Raven straightened up his back and shrugged. "Ah! Well
now, we'll forget such matters as assault and arson and
stick to the subversion of justice. That's the way the lawyers

will refer to what you've been up to. Conspiracy to subvert the course of justice. Think about it."

Jubal did so and reasoned that you couldn't conspire with yourself, which meant that there must be a case against Denton. The ground shifted beneath him. "Bullshit," he said. "You've got nothing."

"Against you, plenty. Less against Denton. You drove an innocent man to suicide, Smiler."

"Innocent?" Jubal's indignation was genuine. "How do you mean, innocent. You've got to be joking!"

Raven's expression changed. "Are you saying that he wasn't innocent?"

"You're bleedin' right, I am. Macfarlane knew that painting was crooked. He'd dabbled and earned before. The only difference this time was that he was conned. He was a mug."

"A mug," repeated Raven. "But you did set him up?"

"I'm not admitting nothing," Jubal said obstinately.

Raven looked at his nails. His grip on the thirty-eight never slackened. "Let's get one thing straight, shall we? Are you willing to give me Denton or do you want to play the hero?"

Jubal's eyes were sly. "A deal?"

Raven shook his head. "Whichever way you look at it, you're in trouble. I think I can put you inside and there are fifty heavies out there on the street who'll be looking to put a hole in your head the moment the news breaks that you're a nark. It's too late for Venezuela."

Jubal was staring at the floor but he took in everything in the room. Everything he needed to run with was in Raven's hip pocket and the gun was between them.

"Then why should I talk?" he said, glancing up. "What have I got to gain?"

Raven leaned forward again. "I've known thieves that I respected. But you're just a piece of shit, the sort of scum that I used to enjoy putting inside. You betray your own kind but Denton betrays the people he's supposed to defend. He's an affront to every cop who does his job decently. I can't get him without you."

Jubal was sweating. "Exactly. And you expect me to give you what you want for nothing, is that it?"

"No. I'm offering you a chance. I'm willing to forget whatever's between you and me. I'm not saying it's easy but I'll do it. I'm talking about what happened last night and before. I want two things from you. A statement made in front of Macfarlane's lawyer and evidence that will tie-in Denton. The testimony of a fellow conspirator isn't enough by itself. It has to be corroborated."

Jubal wiped the back of his neck. "You're asking me to turn Queen's Evidence."

Raven smiled thinly. "Why not? You've been putting people away all your life by the sound of it."

"And all I've got is your word?"

"That's right," said Raven. "You're putting all your eggs in one basket and giving it to me to carry. I'm leaving this house in thirty seconds. You'd better make up your mind whether you're coming with me or staying here."

Jubal shook his head. "Shit, I don't have no real option."

"No," said Raven and came to his feet.

10. John Raven

THE LONG ROAD ran parallel to the park palisades. On one side were the houses, no two alike but each set in the required five acres. Streetlamps alternating with lime trees shed circles of yellow light that were edged with deep shadow. Opposite the houses was the golf course, its sand traps glimmering in the velvet darkness.

Kirstie had been at the wheel since they had left the houseboat. It was the first time she had driven him and he was completely relaxed. She drove as he liked to be driven, her decisions swift and well-judged. He pointed ahead.

"It's the next house but one, the red-brick. The one with all the lights on. Drive past and turn at the end of the road."

She made her turn well beyond the last house. There were no more streetlamps. Park and golf course merged into one, divided only by a paling fence. Kirstie stopped the motor and switched off the lights. He could just see her face, its expression boyish and anxious.

"Are you scared?" she asked curiously.

He moved his shoulders without knowing it. "I don't think so, no. In fact, I'm sure of it. There's only one thing that scares me these days and maybe I shouldn't talk about that."

"Say it anyway," she said.

He took her hand. "I wouldn't want to lose you."

Her fingers tightened on his. "That isn't likely. But I do want you to be careful."

"I try," he said. "Every minute of the day I try. Do you know what your hair looks like in this light?"

He felt her move. "Like butter. You've said it before. It isn't the most romantic statement."

He kissed her throat just below her ear. "I shouldn't be too long. Keep your eyes on those white-painted gates and the moment you see me appear, sprint! OK?"

She nodded quickly. "I wish I didn't worry about you so much. What happens if this man refuses to come with you?"

He unfastened the glove compartment and took out the snub-nosed thirty-eight. He left the catch on safety and tucked the gun in his waistband.

"He'll come," he assured her. "One way or another."

He reached behind and took the plastic bag from the back seat. The half-raw liver inside slithered obscenely. "Keep your cool," he warned. "If I'm not out in an hour's time, make for the nearest phone and call Jerry."

He left the car and walked the couple of hundred yards to Jubal's house. Every window but one at the front was lit. Protective bars identified this as the nursery. There were lights on above the front door and outside the garage. A silver-colored Jaguar was parked next to the Volkswagen he had previously noticed. None of the curtains in the house was drawn. He could see through into the rooms but there was no sign of movement. Nothing but this blaze of light, as though whoever was inside was awaiting his arrival. He opened the five-barred gate and replaced the latch with caution. His sneakers made no noise on the hardtop or the concrete floor of the garage. He drew his gloves on and squatted by the door to the garden. He couldn't hear the dog on the other side but he sensed that the animal was there. Silent, quivering, and ready.

He took a slice of liver in his fingers, pushed it through a small crack in the door, and held it there gingerly. Nothing happened for a second or so, then the meat was removed from his fingers very delicately. He offered another slice to the Doberman. It was taken with the same gentleness. He straightened up and opened the door completely. The Doberman was standing on the pathway, its head cocked expectantly, its one good eye watching Raven. He fed the dog another slice and closed the garden door. The lights were on at the back of the house as well, but two of the upstairs rooms were curtained. The lawn and flower beds were illuminated, and the pool at the end of the garden. Raven hurled the rest of the liver as far as he could. The Doberman bounded after it and was nuzzling the plastic bag as Raven let himself through the open kitchen door. He turned the key and put it in his pocket. It was a large kitchen with many stainless steel and aluminum fittings. Four large control panels had been set into the walls. A full bottle of tonic water stood on top of the refrigerator, the door of which was open. There was a tray with the remains of a meal on the table.

Voices sounded beyond a door at the far end of the room, a woman's voice and a man's. Raven pulled out the gun and thumbed-off the safety catch. He threw the door open suddenly and followed the gun into the hallway. The woman he had seen earlier was sitting on the bottom stair and plainly drunk. Between her and the front door was Jubal. It was easy to recognize him from the insurance company's pictures in spite of the attempt at disguise. He was standing quite still as though pole-axed and about to fall. The look on his face was one of pure shock.

Raven ignored the woman, telling Jubal to empty his pockets. The haul was something that he never had expected. Jubal's passport, an air ticket to Caracas for the following day, and some sort of unofficial letter of credit. It looked as though Raven had arrived just in time.

He knew that he'd have no trouble now, looking at Jubal. The man was smiling and grimacing but his eyes told the truth. He was defeated, with nowhere to go except where he was told. The woman spoke and Raven turned his head, listening to her outburst.

". . . a dirty rotten police-informer!"

Her tear-stained face was bitter and Raven was sorry for her. It was the distilled knowledge of years, acquired painfully by adding hints to denials. She must have finally learned the truth without even wanting to. He watched as she swung her hand at her husband's face and Raven understood. She made her way upstairs shakily. As soon as she had gone, Raven opened the nearest door, cut the lights, and drew the curtains. He switched a light on again. They were in a sort of library. He sat Jubal in a chair and put the facts to him. He had Jubal's papers. It was too late to run and too late to lie. Jubal's only hope was to cooperate. Raven knew that his harangue was 75 percent bluff. He had no real proof, nothing that would stand up in a court of law. But he knew instinctively that Jubal would betray Denton and anyone else, given the opportunity. And in destroying Denton he would destroy himself. It was obvious by now that Denton wasn't in it for the money. He was in it for the power and the glory. It all checked with what Raven already knew about the man and what Jerry had said. But Denton was no less crooked, a cop with no thought other than a record for successful arrests and convictions. It didn't matter how these were obtained, how many innocent men rotted in jail as long as Denton moved on and up.

"You'd better make up your mind whether you're coming with me or staying here," Raven repeated.

"I don't have no real option," Jubal answered sullenly.

Raven had a short word with him in the hallway on the way out. "Look," he said. "I don't like you. I don't like a single thing about you, so behave."

Jubal's smile could have been a sneer. Raven grabbed him quickly and shoved him against the wall. Jubal's eyes popped as Raven's thumb found the artery and pressed on it.

"Wipe that grin off your face and listen," Raven said in a tight voice. "You're getting a break you don't deserve. But I can still pull the plug on you."

He let Jubal go, sickened by the venom his rage had engendered. "You're going to get into a car," he said wearily. "And you're going to sit in the back with me. If you try anything, you're finished. Do you understand?"

Jubal shook his head, his eyes fearful as he massaged his throat. "I understand," he croaked.

They walked down the steps together. The thirty-eight was hidden but Jubal knew where it was, in Raven's pocket. The side-lights of the Citroën showed as the car ghosted toward them. Raven opened the rear door.

"In!" he ordered and followed. Kirstie twisted her body in the driver's seat and took a long hard stare at Jubal. She said nothing, just stared.

"Let's get going," said Raven. He looked out through the trees as they passed the house. The lights were still burning but a blind had been lowered in one of the upstairs rooms. They drove in silence, Jubal with his head turned away, clenching and unclenching the fingers of his right hand. Once he asked for a cheroot. Raven gave him the pack and a light. His mistrust of Jubal was complete. The only way to handle the man was to stay on top of him, give him no room to maneuver, ride him.

Kirstie backed the Citroën into the alleyway. It was almost midnight. The pub was shut but lights inside showed that the staff were still clearing up. Someone had been using the hose on the beer garden, the scent from the rose bushes was strong. The seats had been stacked on the tables.

"Right," said Raven, taking advantage of a gap in the traffic to cross the road. They descended the steps to Belasus' boat. There was no sign of the Californian or his dog. They crossed the deck to the plank that linked the two craft. Lashed as it was at both ends, there was a difference in the levels of the two decks. The crossing looked hazardous and Jubal's face was apprehensive. The smell of scorched wood was still strong.

"Welcome aboard," said Raven. "And don't lose your balance."

Jubal took the plank at the run, arms semaphoring wildly. Kirstie and Raven went after him. Kirstie unlocked the sitting-room door with her own key. She pressed the curtain button and went straight through to Raven's bedroom. Raven locked and bolted the door to the deck. He pulled the gun out again.

"Now listen," he said to Jubal. "You're staying here tonight. It's up to you what happens tomorrow."

Jubal nodded. He was still smiling from habit but his eyes were never still. Raven prodded him through the guest room and into the bathroom. "Do whatever you have to do," said Raven.

Mirrors reflected Jubal's towhead at three different angles. "How about a drink?" he asked.

"Use the tap," said Raven. He watched as Jubal leaned over the hand basin. Raven leaned against the door while Jubal turned his back. "Pull the plug," instructed Raven.

The curtains were drawn in the guest room. "Take off your shoes," said Raven. Jubal eased his neat feet out of his Gucci loafers. "Face down on the bed!" ordered Raven. He took the two pairs of handcuffs from the drawer. They were the old-fashioned type and locked with a screw key. He fastened Jubal's wrists behind his back and then his ankles. He stepped back, looked down.

"Don't waste your time trying to get those off or you'll wind up with no flesh on your wrists."

The bathroom door was already shut. He closed the one that led to the sitting room after him. It was five minutes to midnight. He fixed himself a Scotch-and-water, sat down at the phone, and dialed Lassiter's home number. The lawyer answered the call.

"It's me," said Raven and identified himself. "I need both advice and action. We've already discussed the subject matter."

"Yes," said Lassiter. It was an inquiry rather than an affirmation. "I see."

"It's important," said Raven. "I don't want to waste your time or mine but Macfarlane *was* framed. And I've got what's necessary to prove it."

"Yes," repeated Lassiter. "And you'd like to see me, is that it?"

"Right," said Raven.

"How about nine-thirty tomorrow morning at my office? Could you make it by then?"

"Yes," said Raven. "I'll have someone else with me."

"I understand," said the lawyer. "Nine-thirty then."

Raven put the light out and finished his drink sitting in the darkness. His mind was on what Jubal had said about Macfarlane. It was easy enough to credit even on the basis of what Kirstie had told him of her brother's travels. It seemed that he'd taken the Hippie Trail west from Katmandu, driving other peoples' cars overland, teaching English in Teheran, selling his blood in Athens. He had fetched up in Amsterdam, young, with a good appearance and a bankroll from somewhere. Whether he was in business for himself or just fronting for others it would have been easy for him to buy the odd stolen article in one of the London street markets, take it back to Holland and sell at a good profit. All of which made him an ideal mark. Only those with larceny in their hearts could be conned. And conned he probably had been. The problem was whether or not to tell Kirstie what Jubal had said. Chances were that she wouldn't believe him anyway. Raven took his empty glass into the kitchen. The lights were out in the bedroom when he went through to brush his teeth. There was no sound from the guest room. He opened his windows wide, catching whatever there was of the night breeze. He felt his way to the bed to find the sheet turned back in anticipation of his arrival. He climbed in beside Kirstie, her bare flesh warm against him. He liked the touch of her, her firm breasts and hard flat muscles under the suntanned skin. She moved her head to his chest.

"Why did you bring that man here?"

He pushed his fingers through her hair. "What else would I have done with him?"

She stirred. "I don't know. It's just that everything that you're doing seems to be against the law. It scares me."

"Don't let it," he answered. "If we blow this, that's the time to worry. Success wipes the slate clean. Incidentally —and don't jump down my throat—did you ever think that Jamie just might be guilty?"

Her body stiffened in his arms. "How do you mean, guilty? He was framed. You said so yourself."

"I said he'd been framed. That's different. He could still have been guilty and framed."

She wriggled out of his arms and put the width of the bed between them. Her voice was sad. "Don't you believe in anyone or anything?"

"I believe in you and me," he replied. "That's why I want you to face what just might be the truth. Jubal's going to testify that Jamie knew that painting was stolen. It won't make any difference to what happens to Denton. My concern is how much difference it will make to you."

"Will it be the truth?" she asked quietly. "I mean what Jubal says."

"I think so," he answered. "It doesn't matter to Jubal one way or the other."

The movement of the bed told him that she was crying and he reached out, taking her in his arms. "Listen to me, darling," he said. "Jamie gave up. He just didn't want to go on living. Five years is a long time for someone who's never seen the inside of a jail. Nearly two thousand days and nights. The prospect could have been too daunting. On the other hand, it might have been that he couldn't face you, knowing the truth himself, couldn't go on living a lie."

She held him very tightly, saying nothing, but hiding her wet face against his chest. He stayed as he was till her breathing was deep and regular.

Morning came all too quickly. Raven swung his legs out of bed, picked his robe from the floor, and went through to the guest room. Jubal was lying with his face turned sideways on the pillow. His eyes were open but red, his chin sprouting stubble. Raven unfastened the cuffs. Jubal sat up, groaning as he massaged his wrists and ankles.

"Like a bleedin' animal you're treating me," he complained.

"That's right," said Raven. "An animal that's not to be trusted."

Jubal shook his head, running his finger round the inside of his collar. "I don't know what you're scared of. Where am I supposed to run to?"

Raven drew the curtains on a perfect summer day. Blue skies, the river calm, a faint breeze. He heard Kirstie turn the key in the bathroom. He sat on the bed next to Jubal's.

"How many times did you pull this stunt with Denton? I mean setting people up?"

Jubal wriggled his shoulders. "I'm not sure. Ten, twelve, maybe."

The whisper of wind through the open window carried the tang of tidal water. Raven scratched his chin, looking at the other man.

"Who found the jobs?"

"Me *and* Denton. It all depended. I mean, sometimes he knew where the gear was. Sometimes it was me. It was the same with finding a customer. There were times when Denton supplied one, someone whose collar he wanted to feel. Other times he left it to me."

"But it was always you who claimed the reward money. Didn't Denton ever want his end?"

Jubal had one leg over the other, rubbing an ankle again. "You've got the wrong ideas about Denton, mate. You're going to have to get them straight, you're going to make this thing stick with him. Denton never took as much as a fucking cigar from nobody. He's too smart for that. What Denton wants is an office with *Assistant Commissioner* wrote on the door. He told me that, years ago."

Water rattled against the shower curtains in the bathroom. It was almost seven-thirty. They were due at the lawyer's office in a couple of hours' time.

"Who sent those thugs the other night? Whose idea was it?" Raven demanded.

"Denton's," Jubal said promptly. "*And* the fire!"

Raven changed tack. "You know I used to be on the Force?"

A picture frame slid across the top of the tallboy as the *Albatross* wallowed in the wake from a passing tugboat. "Yes, I heard," said Jubal.

Raven showed his teeth. "What I mean is that I still have contacts. They'll be looking for you at the ports if you have any ideas about running."

"Why don't you give it a rest?" Jubal said wearily. "I ain't running *nowhere*. I've got nothing to run with, have I? You offered me a deal and I've taken it."

"A chance," amended Raven. "No deal."

Jubal cocked his head. "It's not the same thing?"

"Not the same thing at all," answered Raven. Kirstie was out in the kitchen. Raven gave Jubal a disposable razor and the freedom of the bathroom. He went out and had words with Kirstie. She was wearing her hair tied back, her loafers, and a yellow linen dress. She looked scrubbed, determined, and desirable. Bacon and eggs were cooking in the pan and there was coffee brewing.

"I'm not eating with that man," she announced.

"You don't have to," he answered. "He can eat in here. We'll have ours in the sitting room."

Jubal came into the kitchen. His clothes were creased but the rest of him was neat and tidy. He wrinkled his nose as he smelled the food and rubbed his palms together. Kirstie put egg, bacon, and toast on a plate and slammed it down on the kitchen table. She set another tray and carried their meal through.

"I hate him," she said viciously. "Sitting there, grinning and rubbing his hands like some friend of the family."

"It's only for another hour," said Raven.

She poured his coffee, added cream and sugar. "And what happens then?"

He was still in his robe and unshaven. "I don't know yet. But he won't be coming back here, that's for sure."

He shaved with both bathroom doors open, his ears alert. The thirty-eight was on a shelf in front of him, pinning down the papers he had taken from Jubal. He dressed in his jeans, sneakers, and blue cotton shirt. Kirstie and Jubal had changed places when he went out, Kirstie doing the washing up, Jubal in the sitting room with a cheroot. Raven helped himself to a Caporal and scribbled Denton's home number on a scrap of paper. He placed it by the telephone. It was twenty minutes past eight.

"He'll be there now. Call him. Say that you've got to see him this afternoon."

Doubt flared in Jubal's eyes. "He won't do it, mate. I mean he already told me. 'You're on your own,' he said."

Raven lifted the phone off its stand. "He'll do it. Tell him that I just called you at home. Tell him I said that I've got positive evidence that links the two of you." He shoved the phone toward Jubal.

Jubal looked down at it suspiciously. "What evidence?"

"Never mind," said Raven. "You don't know. I wouldn't tell you. I've told you that I have to see you."

Jubal dialed. He was starting to sweat even as the number began ringing. The conversation was short and one-sided. Jubal put the phone back and mopped at his neck with his handkerchief.

"Four o'clock, Speakers' Corner. '*Be* there,' he said. He'll find me."

The choice of venue was one that Raven appreciated. You could drive there, leave your car in the underground park, and walk a hundred yards to Speakers' Corner. Once there, you had a clear field of vision all the way around.

Jubal's eyes slid sideways. "What's all this in aid of, anyway?"

"Later," said Raven. Kirstie had come into the sitting room. "Let's go," he said.

They rode as before, Kirstie driving, Raven and Jubal in back. It was still early and they found an empty metered space on Bute Street. Kirstie waited in the car with a newspaper. The two men climbed the stairs. They waited in the outer office. Jubal's mouth and eyes were tense. The girl there had had a late night and showed it. She stifled a yawn with difficulty.

"Will you come this way, please." She showed them into the room with the dried flowers, dirty carpet, and scattered papers. The window was on the west side of the building and open. Flypapers attached to the ceiling lifted in the currents of air. Lassiter rose to greet them, dapper in a pin-stripe suit and bow tie. The reading spectacles he removed were the same shade of ginger as his eyebrows and hair. Raven made the introduction.

"This is John Jubal. What he wants is to make a statement about his part in a conspiracy to frame Jamie Macfarlane."

"Ah," said Lassiter, and gave Jubal the benefit of a prolonged inspection. "Well, now, I have been told the gist of your statement, your *proposed* statement, and it's my duty to put forward certain possible consequences. I have to be sure that you are fully aware of your legal position."

Jubal's smile was suddenly vacant. "I'm not with you."

"Right," Lassiter said briskly. "I'll explain. An affirmation made under oath is a serious undertaking. Once it has been made and your signature affixed your statement will be investigated by the authorities. Should charges subsequently be brought against any person or persons, you might be required to give evidence in a court of law."

Jubal looked from Lassiter to Raven. "What *is* all this? You didn't say nothing about appearing in no court. You know I can't do that."

Raven shrugged. "Don't take things literally. Mr. Lassiter has to put these matters to you."

Jubal's face was a shade paler than before. "What I want to know is whether or not I'm going to be nicked."

Lassiter's pale eyebrows drew together. "It's not going to be as straightforward as that, I'm afraid. It would be up to the Director of Public Prosecutions to determine your position. He might feel disposed to admit your testimony as 'Queen's Evidence,' which would mean that no criminal charge would be brought against you. And then again he might not. He might take the view that your statement was a confession to a series of illegal acts. It's entirely at his discretion."

Jubal blinked rapidly at Raven. "What sort of chance is that? I don't like the sound of any of this."

Raven leaned forward, his patience at an end. His sense of affront was strong. This weasel had no right to treat for terms.

"You came here to make a statement," said Raven. "And that's what you're going to do. If not, you have my word that I'll see you put in a cage."

Jubal turned his plea to the lawyer, who spread his hands. "It's entirely up to you," said Lassiter.

The fight appeared to go from Jubal and his face was sullen instead of smiling. "All right," he said. "Let's get it over."

Lassiter looked at his watch. "There should be someone here by now." He spoke into the box on his desk. A dark girl wearing spectacles came in with a Speedo pen and a note pad. She sat down, crossed her legs, and rested the pad on her knee. Everyone looked at Jubal, who was showing no enthusiasm.

"Come on," said Raven. "Your name, age, and address. Start where Denton gets in touch with you about the painting."

Jubal licked his lips. He released the words reluctantly, dropping his voice whenever his narrative led him onto dangerous ground. A couple of times the girl had to ask him to speak up. He did so like a man who agrees to do his duty in difficult circumstances.

He came to the end of his story. Lassiter consulted his watch again. "How long will this take to type up, Joan?"

The girl flicked through the pages of her notebook. "I'd say about ten minutes. How many copies do you need?"

"A top and two carbons should do it," said Raven.

The three men sat in silence as the electric typewriter clattered along the corridor. The girl came back into the room and placed the neatly stapled pages in front of the lawyer. Once she had gone, Lassiter donned his spectacles and read the statement through. He glanced across at Raven.

"You realize that none of this is going to stand up against Denton. I mean in court, of course. All he has to do is make a blanket denial."

Raven nodded. "That's being take care of. Suppose that I give you a tape-recording of a conversation between Denton and Jubal. Something that *will* stand up in court. Evidence of a criminal conspiracy to frame Macfarlane."

"Where is it?" asked Lassiter.

"I don't have it yet. But what do you think?"

Lassiter pondered. "I'm not sure," he admitted. "But if the evidence is strong enough Denton certainly wouldn't survive a disciplinary investigation. There is one other thing. Jamie's dead. The only way to clear his name would be by means of a Public Inquiry. If we *did* wreck Denton, the Home Secretary would have to agree to one. He'd have no alternative."

Raven's voice was quiet, the noise of the traffic outside suddenly very loud.

"Macfarlane never saw inside that package but he knew what it was. He was buying stolen property and he was fully aware of it." He looked across the room. "At least that's what Jubal says. I believe him."

Lassiter touched the stapled papers in front of him. "There's nothing about it in his statement."

"Maybe he's bashful," said Raven. The truth, he knew, was that Jubal had had time to think things over. Since Kirstie Macfarlane was Raven's lady, it might be better to soft-pedal her brother's involvement.

"*Is* this true?" Lassiter asked Jubal.

Jubal looked at Raven for a lead and drew a blank. "What it is here," he said bitterly "is that I'm supposed to be the bleedin' villain and everyone else is a boy scout. Of *course* Macfarlane knew! He thought he was going to pay two fucking grand, didn't he, for a painting worth a hundred and twelve!"

"Have you told his sister?" Lassiter was speaking to Raven. Raven nodded. "And?" asked Lassiter.

"They were close. But not as close as she thought they were. She'll get over it."

Lassiter put the typescript in a drawer. "You realize that this means there can be no question of a Public Inquiry?"

"Forget about justice," said Raven. "I'm talking about expediency. Denton's a crooked cop and I want his hide."

Lassiter's gaze left the room and settled somewhere beyond the open windows. "How are you going to get this tape-recording?" he said at last.

Raven pushed his chair back. "I didn't hear that question. But if I get it, will you go to the Commissioner?"

Lassiter took a long deep breath and held it before exhaling. "I *can't* forget about justice. Jamie's involvement will have to be incorporated into Mr. Jubal's testimony and he will have to sign it. I'm afraid there's no time now. I'll be in court all day. Give me a ring at home this evening." He was on his feet.

Raven followed suit. "You didn't give me an answer. Will you go to the Commissioner?"

"Justice *and* expediency," said Lassiter. "Yes, I'll go."

Raven escorted Jubal down the stairs to the car. Bute Street was filling with early shoppers and vehicles were beginning to be double-parked.

"We'd better get out of here," said Kirstie, swinging round and pushing the hair from her face.

"Everything's under control," said Raven.

Kirstie's avoidance of Jubal was studious. Not once did she look at him. "I'd like to go over to Louise's apartment. That's unless you need me for anything."

"A good idea," said Raven, and smiled at the man beside him. "Jubal and I are tight. We understand one another." He was smiling but there was no humor in his voice. "I've got a feeling that he's going to be a folk hero. They'll be writing ballads about him."

Jubal tried an uncertain grin but thought better of it. "Get Louise to call Jerry," said Raven. "I'd like a complete rundown on where he'll be for the next forty-eight hours. OK?"

Kirstie moved her head up and down. "How much do I tell her?"

"Louise?" Raven gave it some thought. "As little as possible. If she asks awkward questions, say you don't know." He winked at Jubal, who sighed resignedly.

Kirstie moved over and Raven took the driver's seat. "I told Lassiter what Jubal said about Jamie."

Her eyes searched his. "Did he believe it?"

"Accept, believe." Raven threw a hand. "Yes, I think he believed it. What about you, do you believe it?"

Neither of them as much as glanced back at Jubal. Kirstie didn't speak but her look gave Raven his answer. "I'll see you at three," he said. "Back on the boat."

She flagged down a passing cab. Raven motioned Jubal into the passenger seat. "You're doing fine so far. Do you want to call your wife, tell her you're in good hands?"

Jubal massaged a chafed wrist, his expression resentful. "I wish you'd get off my back. Why does everything have to be a bleedin' joke with you?"

"It doesn't," said Raven. "I appreciate the serious side of life. That's why I want you to listen to me very carefully. I won't be very far away when you go to meet Denton and I'll be recording every word that's said. We'll only have the one chance so we've got to get it right. Is that quite clear?"

"Yes, it's clear," Jubal said sourly.

Raven put the car in motion. He drove north across the park, taking the carriageway. He could see the bandstand off to his left, down in a hollow. Trees nearby afforded plenty of cover. Halfway out on Edgware Road he stopped at the Star of India Electronic Mart. A Hindu salesman sold Raven a tiny Japanese transmitter. It had a minute wire mast and was powered by a PP3 battery. Signals went out on the 102 megahertz frequency and had a range up to three hundred yards. A combined receiver-recorder completed the unit. Back in the car, Raven emptied his cigarette pack of its contents and fitted the small transmitter in their place.

"Put it in your pocket," he told Jubal and inspected the result. "Perfect," he said. "That's your new toy."

He drove to the top of Hampstead Heath where he stopped the car. An Italian was selling Coke and hamburgers from a stand. Raven bought two orders. They ate, sitting on a bench.

"Right," said Raven when they had finished. He led the way toward the pond, talking as they went. The sun was high. A small hawk circled lazily somewhere between the sun and the earth. "We're going to try this thing out," said Raven. "I'll be in those trees over there. You stay by the pond. You can move about if you like but keep talking. It doesn't have to be loud. Just use your normal voice."

Jubal didn't seem too happy. "What am I supposed to talk about?"

Raven took him by the forearm. "Think about Macfarlane and think about me and talk to Denton about it. That's what you're going to have to do later, you prick, so you might as well get in some practice."

Jubal walked off, red-faced and muttering. Raven walked into the shade of the oak trees and lay down on the grass. There was no fear of Jubal's running. The man was completely demoralized. Raven no longer had any real interest in Jubal. Denton was his prey. Denton represented everything Raven loathed on the Force. A villain masquerading as an honest cop, immune to a bribe but stealing the liberty of innocent men. Raven rolled over on his stomach and switched on the receiver-recorder. The spools started to revolve. Raven gave it ten minutes then played the tape back. Jubal's voice was startlingly clear, launched in some virulent self-accusation that embraced Denton and his own stupidity. Raven switched off the set and called Jubal back to base.

"Not bad," said Raven. "But you'll have to feed Denton the right lines. We want a confession, remember."

Jubal waited till a couple of women had passed. He was sweating again and flustered. "You people are crazy, all of you! Denton's no mug. If he catches on to what's happening, he's going to do me a mischief, that's a certainty."

"He won't catch on," said Raven. "Just keep that cigarette packet in your pocket and act normally."

"Again with the normal!" Jubal's voice sounded hysterical. "You must be bleedin' joking!"

"*Normally*," Raven reiterated. "You're *supposed* to be nervous. I'm breathing down your neck and you want to know what to do about it."

Jubal lit a cheroot with shaking fingers. "I got no chance at all, do I? When are you going to let me go?"

"As soon as your statement's signed and the tape's in the proper hands."

Jubal's eyes were furtive. "Do I get my passport back?"

"You sleep in your own bed," said Raven. "That's already a start."

Three o'clock and they were back on the boat. There was a note from Mrs. Burrows on the kitchen table. The builders had quoted for the repairs. Raven called the firm and agreed to the price. A spokesman assured him that work would start in a couple of days. Raven gave Jubal the beer he asked for. Jubal carried it out on deck and sat there staring down over the side. Raven changed his clothes, putting on respectable trousers and a sports jacket, a straw hat, and sunglasses. A cab stopped up on the Embankment. Raven looked through the kitchen window. Kirstie was coming down the steps. Saul and the dog were in the Herborium. Raven went to meet her. She took his hand at the end of the plank, her face puzzled.

"For God's sake, you look like a tourist."

He grinned. "That's exactly what I'm supposed to look like."

Jubal was still aft, intent on the water. Raven followed Kirstie into the sitting room. She untied the ribbon and shook her hair free.

"What's the matter with him?" she asked, nodding in Jubal's direction.

"He's starting to get nervous."

She poured herself a glass of tonic water. "How about you, are you getting nervous?"

He shrugged and then shook his head. "No more than usual. How was Louise?"

Kirstie put her glass down. She opened her handbag, answering as she did a fresh job with her lipstick.

"She's worried sick. In fact, they both are. They know perfectly well that there's more going on than we're saying."

"Did you ask about Jerry?"

She put the lipstick and hand mirror back in her bag. "They're in tonight. Jerry's got a judo class tomorrow evening. Louise is rehearsing something for Taiwan Television."

"Great," said Raven. To know where Jerry was gave him a sense of security.

She watched as he went to the desk. "What are you doing now?" she asked curiously.

He had brought the gun from the car. He locked it away in a drawer together with Jubal's passport and papers.

"The art of self-defense," he said. "The trick is, only use when necessary." He came across the room and kissed her on the nape of her neck. "Mmm! I love that smell. My sweetheart, you're going to have to stay down in the car-park."

She twisted out of his grasp. "In the *car-park?* Then why am I going at all?"

He cocked his head on one side. "*A* because I like your company and *B* because I may need you to drive."

He showed her the small recorder. "Jubal's got the other half of this. We've been up on Hampstead Heath, practicing. It'll work."

She lit a cigarette and sat on the sofa, displaying a warm brown length of thigh. "I told Louise about Jamie. She understands."

He started a smoke of his own. "Just what does she understand?"

She moved a shoulder. "That Jamie still shouldn't have died."

The look in her eyes disturbed him. "You didn't tell her about Denton?"

She shook her head. "I did no such thing, John. I said that we'd found out that Jamie was involved in that business somehow and that there was no longer any question of clearing his name."

He blew smoke, conscious of everything that she wasn't saying, how much the admission meant to her. "*I* understand as well, you know, Kirstie."

She smiled with her whole face, looking suddenly happier than he had ever seen her.

"I do know. That's why I love you."

They were in the vast car-park beneath Marble Arch. It was quarter to four. Raven gave Jubal his last-minute instructions. As soon as he was through with Denton, Jubal was to return to the car, making sure that he hadn't been followed. Raven checked the batteries on the set and trial-ran the spools.

"OK," he said. "Move!"

Kirstie nodded as Jubal walked toward the nearest exit. "That could be the last we see of him!"

They were sixty feet beneath the trees, grass, and sunshine. Strobe lamps lit acres of parked cars. "He'll be back," said Raven. "Rats are the arch-survivors." He touched her hand and went after Jubal.

He put his sunglasses on again at the top of the ramp, dazzled by the sudden glare. Speakers' Corner was three hundred yards east of where he had surfaced, a space of hardtop the size of a football field and bounded by iron railings. The place was invaded by self-publicists on Saturdays and Sundays, soapbox orators who spoke in English, Persian, Arabic, and Urdu. Special Branch officers drifted through the crowds along with the pickpockets. The police took notes and used their concealed cameras. The speeches varied from the straight Anarchist and Marxist ticket to "Hang the Left" messages, pleas for truth through belief in a flat world and for sanity with a nut diet. It was an escape route, a safety valve, but today it was almost deserted. The park was green and inviting, the expanse of hardtop arid. The only people beyond the railings were a man with two dogs and Jubal. A worried Jubal, moving from place to place, with constant looks over his shoulder.

Raven made his way south toward a stand selling ice cream and tea. Deck chairs were stacked at the side. He took one from the pile and carried it twenty yards. Then he opened it and sat down, legs sprawled, facing Speakers' Corner. The receiver in his lap looked like a small transistor radio. A man came from the trees as Raven watched and walked toward Jubal. It was Denton. Raven switched on and the spools started to revolve. The sound was clear above the background noise of traffic, Denton's voice first.

"You're asking for trouble, you know. I thought I made it very plain to you. No more meetings."

Jubal's voice was surly. "What did you expect me to do? This was supposed to be a straightforward bit of business. No comebacks, no problems, you said, and I believed you. A Detective-Inspector on the Flying Squad ought to know the score, I thought. Then all of a sudden, the shit starts hitting the fan."

Denton sounded the cooler of the two. "Let's stick to Raven. What about Raven?"

"I've been a fool," whined Jubal. "But he got me off guard and you didn't want to know. He's got those pictures the insurance people took of me and the receipt for the money. And he says he's got something on you."

An ambulance siren drowned out the beginning of Denton's reply. The tape picked up at ". . . about me. He's bluffing. What's this about a statement?"

"That's what I meant," said Jubal. "He got me off guard. Showed up at the house with a gun and forced me into his car. That bleedin' girl was driving, Macfarlane's sister."

"How did he get your address?"

"How the fuck would I know?" said Jubal. "Look, I don't care what you say. You and me's in this together. You're the one who put it up. If it hadn't been for you I wouldn't have heard of no Peter van Eyck painting."

"*Raven,*" said Denton.

"He put the cuffs on me, the bleedin' bracelets! Made me sleep on his boat, then this morning we went to see Macfarlane's lawyer."

"How could you phone me if you were on the boat?"

"When he took the cuffs off this morning, he said I was

free. I'd agreed to go to the lawyer's. I called you the first
chance I had."

"But you *went* to the lawyer's!"

"Yes, but I told them a lot of bullshit."

Raven could see the two men, two hundred yards away,
facing one another.

"Did you mention my name?" asked Denton.

"No!"

"You lying fucker," said Denton. "It's me you've been
telling the bullshit!"

"As God's my judge," said Jubal. "I swear it!"

"Liar," said Denton again.

"Look," said Jubal. "They mentioned your name but I
swore I'd never met you."

"Raven knows you're meeting me, doesn't he?" Denton
said sharply.

"Christ, no! I'm supposed to go back to the lawyer's this
evening and meet Raven there. I've got to sign that statement. The time's come for you to put in some help, mate."

"If you haven't signed it, your statement's not worth
shit."

A police helicopter swooped low across the park, the
noise from its motors making it impossible for Raven to
hear the men's voices. He watched, frustrated, as the chop-
per hovered over the west end of Oxford Street. When he
looked back in the direction of Speakers' Corner, Denton
and Jubal had vanished.

He jumped up and hurried in the direction of Speakers'
Corner. Two uniformed policemen were standing near the
railings; otherwise the enclosed space was empty. There
was no sight of Denton or Jubal on the grass and beyond
that pursuit would be useless. Waves of pedestrians broke
on Marble Arch, spilling into Park Lane and Oxford
Street. Half a dozen subterranean entrances led down to
pedestrian underpasses. The spools were still going around

on the tape-recorder but the only sound he was getting was static. He switched off the set and made his way back to the car. He climbed in beside Kirstie and took off his hat and his sunglasses. He had a sudden sense of foreboding, a feeling that he'd been tricked in some way.

He expressed the feeling to Kirstie. "I think I might have been had."

Her face was anxious in the half-light. "What happened?"

"Well," he said. "I took my eye off them for thirty seconds at the most. There was this police helicopter. When I looked around they were gone."

He suddenly remembered what she had said half an hour before. That could be the last they saw of Jubal. She might well have reminded him of it but didn't. He switched the set on again and played the tape. Kirstie listened, tapping her teeth with a fingernail, till the sound of the voices on the tape changed to the roar of the helicopter motors and then static.

"And they disappeared just like that?"

He nodded. "I didn't have a chance. There were people coming and going in all directions. It was hopeless to look for them."

"So what happens now?"

Footsteps sounded behind them and he turned his head. It wasn't Jubal. The lines of parked cars shone like beetles under the lamps. A sudden thought decided him.

"Let's get back to the boat."

They parked next to the Herborium and hurried down the steps. Saul Belasus called as they crossed his deck but Raven kept going. He ran across the plank and opened the sitting-room door. The thought at the back of his head had been that Jubal might have seen him lock away the papers, passport, and gun, that Jubal had doubled back and retrieved them. But the desk was just as Raven had left it. He took a deep breath and let it go with relief.

"He might still be back," he said defensively. "Something could have come up."

"I'll make some tea," Kirstie said quickly. Raven stood at the starboard windows, watching the steps leading down from the Embankment. Jubal had chosen an odd time to defect if he had defected. Raven was still standing at the window long after he had finished his tea. He could just see Kirstie's brown bare legs up on the bed through the open doorway. It was twenty minutes to six and quiet down on the river. The thunder of the homebound traffic above passed over their heads. He left the windows and went to the desk. He put Jubal's papers in an envelope, stamped it, and addressed it to his bank. There was a mailbox thirty yards away. He dropped the envelope inside and walked back to the *Albatross*. Saul was still in his wheelhouse. Raven lifted a hand as the Californian waved.

Kirstie was on the bed, the sunshine slanting across her face. She opened her eyes, shading them with her hand.

"I wish you'd relax," she said.

He sat down beside her. "I can't. Something's gone wrong and I don't know what it is."

She rolled sideways with a sudden movement, taking his hand between hers. "Why don't we just forget the whole thing? Tell the police and then take the first plane out. I want you to see my flat. I want you to walk through Paris with me."

He squeezed her fingers but said nothing. *"Please,"* she asked. "I love you and I'm scared. I don't want anything terrible to happen to us."

He looked down at her face, reading her eyes. If he had any sense he would do as she said. He did his best to make her understand.

"I can't, Kirstie. I know how you feel. But it's all very different now because of Jamie, Kirstie. People like Denton are important to me. He's evil and should be exposed. In a sense it's my duty. I just can't walk away from it. Don't you see this, darling?"

"I see all too clearly," she said, coming up on an elbow. "It isn't the ladies in your past that I have to worry about, it's your goddam sense of duty."

He shrugged. "I have to do it, Kirstie."

"Do *what*, for crissakes? If you could answer that I wouldn't mind so much. You've been beaten up, people have tried to set fire to us, and you're still trying to be Dick Tracy!"

"Don't be angry with me," he pleaded.

"Angry?" The tears in her eyes were from frustration. "I could kill you myself. You talk about loving me. Does that mean that you *own* me? Am I not supposed to have opinions of my own anymore? You're putting our love at risk and you don't have the right to do it."

He crossed the room to the window, aware of the importance of the moment. Three days had brought new meaning to his life. A wrong decision now could destroy it. He turned to her again.

"Perhaps I shouldn't have talked about duty. I'm sorry. How about revenge? Revenge for the beating up and the fire, revenge for every poor bastard Denton's imprisoned illegally. And that includes Jamie, no matter what his guilty knowledge may have been."

She was up now, sitting on the bed, her hair in disorder. "Let's leave Jamie out of it."

He sensed the hostility in her voice. "Hold it," he said. "You're not giving me a chance to explain myself."

Her expression softened and she held out both hands. "I'm sorry, darling. I'm being beastly to you. Try again!"

He knelt beside her and brought his head close to hers.

"Here's what we do. We wait on the boat until ten o'clock. If Jubal hasn't turned up or phoned by then, I'll call Jerry and do whatever he says should be done. Does that make sense?"

"It does, my lover, it does." She smiled and took his face in her hands. "Meanwhile, lie down beside me."

"Hang on a minute," said Raven. "I've just thought of something."

The idea of Jubal returning to the boat, alone or with somebody else, was still on Raven's mind. He took the snub-nosed gun from the desk and wrapped it in a plastic bag. The fire hadn't touched the port side of the deck, the flower-tubs or roses. Raven buried the gun loosely below the soil. Then he took the tape-recorder and tape to the neighboring boat. Saul Belasus was sitting in the sun reading. He was wearing a coolie hat and a loincloth.

Raven held up the tape-machine. "I want to leave this somewhere safe, Saul."

"Safe?" He slapped a fly off his shoulder. "Help yourself," he said largely.

Raven walked into the wheelhouse and went below. Except where Saul bunked, most of the space was occupied by trays of seedlings. The Californian's clothes hung from a line stretched across the cabin. The Great Dane's bed was near his bunk, a pile of wood shavings enclosed in a rough framework. Raven stuck the tape-recorder under the shavings, patted the Great Dane's head, and went back aloft. Saul twisted, combing his dyed beard.

"It can't be the fuzz, can it?" he asked curiously.

"I wouldn't think so," said Raven, grinning. "But in a world full of trouble, who knows?" He put his finger on his lips, winked and went back to his own boat.

11 . Smiling Jack Jubal

THE POLICE HELICOPTER slipped and dipped over-head like some great dragonfly. The noise of its motors drowned their voices. Denton jerked his head toward the gate in the railings. Jubal followed him through. Anything else would have created suspicion and Jubal had the feeling that he was doing well. The two men walked three hundred yards to where Denton had left his car on the west-bound carriageway. It was a blue Ford without police markings. Denton unlocked the doors and Jubal took the seat beside him. Then, without any warning, Denton pushed his hand out.

"All right, asshole, let's have it!"

The cigarette package in Jubal's pocket took on added weight and dimensions. His arm dropped involuntarily and he grasped the package protectively.

"Let you have *what*, mate?" he asked, blinking.

Denton's fingers snaked out and he closed them on Jubal's wrist. Then he withdrew Jubal's hand and prized the palm open. The cigarette package fell to the floor. Denton retrieved it, opened it, and shook his head. It was as though he had found something amusing. His eyes were oddly bright and he was grinning.

"You bastard," he said, almost affectionately, and shook his head again.

Jubal's palms were clammy. He knew that he had to lie but his built-in fear of Denton inhibited him.

"I couldn't do nothing else," he whined finally. The car had become a capsule removed from reality. People were walking across the grass only a few yards away. Others were eating and talking, lying down. "He came to my house with a gun," he said.

Denton's eyes were definitely strange. He glanced up at the police helicopter as it lifted and peeled off to the south. "A gun," he encouraged. "How did he find out where you lived?"

Jubal's outburst was from the heart. "How the fuck do I know? He walked in, stuck this gun up my bleedin' nose, and made me get into his car. I told you, I had to sleep on his boat last night. Then this morning we went to see Macfarlane's lawyer."

Denton lifted the tiny transmitter. "Where's the other half of this?"

Jubal pointed back at the entrance to the underground car-park. "Raven's got it. He's down there now with that girl."

"Recording every bloody word we said. Asshole!" Denton repeated. "You say the Macfarlane girl is with him?"

Jubal nodded eagerly. "They're living together on his boat."

Denton popped a stick of gum in his mouth. "What was in this statement you say you made? I want the truth, mind! You can cut out the bullshit."

Jubal's hand bounced an invisible ball. "Well—you know! It's a sort of confession. Raven was more or less telling me what to say and some bird was writing it down. How the business with Macfarlane started. All the ins and outs of it."

Denton shifted his gum. "There's nothing like a good clean confession. Then *of course* you mentioned my name."

Jubal was moving cautiously from truth to half-truth to lie, testing each surface carefully.

"I mentioned it, yes. But I never signed the statement."
Denton swooped on the answer. "Is that the truth?"

"On my life!" swore Jubal. "On my mother's life!"

"She's been dead for twenty years," Denton said sourly.
A group of horsemen cantered by on the bridle path but
Denton kept his eyes fixed on Jubal. Finally he spoke. "I
can get myself out of all this without too much trouble and
leave you in the shit. I'm wondering what to do about you."

"Look," Jubal said desperately. "I know I've done wrong
but some of the blame is yours. If only I can get out of the
country there's not much anyone can do. I was all set to go.
Now that fucker has my passport, my ticket, and a letter
that I need. Help me get them back and you've got a friend
for life."

Denton's nose thinned. "*That* I can do without. OK, I've
got an idea. But you're going to have to behave yourself, do
exactly what I say. One wrong move and you're in the
slammer. I can do it and you know that I can do it!"

Jubal wound the window down fully, grateful for the
rush of air on his face and neck. "Them two's expecting
me back at the car."

Denton's smile was foxy. "So much the better. What were
your travel plans?"

Jubal licked his lips. "The plane leaves at twenty minutes
past midnight, tomorrow."

Denton switched on the motor. "Behave yourself as I
said and you'll be on it. It isn't because I like you. It's
because it's neater that way."

Jubal fished for a cheroot. This was nothing short of a
miracle. He was suddenly back where he had started before Raven had invaded the house. Denton made a U-turn,
drove down Park Lane and past Buckingham Palace. Jubal
leaned back comfortably as he realized where they were
going. All the clout and cunning of New Scotland Yard was
about to be invoked on his behalf. Denton stopped the car

near the front entrance to the Yard. He left the car and leaned back through the open window.

"If anyone should ask, I'll be back in five minutes."

He returned, a few seconds better than his promise, and took his seat behind the wheel. He winked at Jubal.

"The ball is in motion."

Jubal grinned, infected by Denton's air of assurance. "You're not going to nick him, are you?" The prospect was exciting.

Denton shook his head. "I've got a better scheme than that. One more call and we'll be in business." He steered away from the curb and east on Victoria Street. He stopped in Cannon Row outside the police station. "This could take a while, you might as well come in."

Jubal climbed out of the car with new confidence. The police station, a small grimy building a hundred years old, was tucked away among the ministries of Whitehall. They walked up the steps to the entrance hall. Denton moved close to Jubal, his voice quiet and confidential.

"I'm going upstairs to the C.I.D. room. Maybe you'd better not be on show. Wait in here for a minute." He opened a door.

It wasn't the first time Jubal had seen the inside of a Detention Room. The walls were bare and smooth, the linoleum on the floor scuffed and scarred with cigarette burns. There were bars on the high window. Jubal perched his buttocks on the edge of the table and lit another cheroot. There was now only one left but Raven had returned his keys and money. He could buy a fresh pack later. He could see officers coming and going in the hallway beyond the open door. The minutes stretched. It was just after five o'clock. He hoped that Denton would soon be through. There were things to be done, a bag to pack. Maybe not the bag, on second thought. That would mean going back to Richmond and another scene with Millie. The faintest of clicks made him turn his head. He saw that the door had just been closed. He stared in disbelief, seeing that there was no handle inside the room. Some clown in the hallway must have closed the door, thinking that the room was empty. Jubal walked across and beat lightly on the door with the flat of his hand.

"Hey! There's someone in here!"

He put his ear to the crack and heard nothing. He banged harder. "Open up!" he shouted. "Open this bleedin' door!"

It was three or four minutes before there was any response. Keys jangled. The door was thrown open suddenly. Two uniformed cops stood outside, Denton behind them.

"All right, mate," said one of the cops. "Pick up your parrots and monkeys and follow me!"

The three men escorted Jubal across the hall and into the Charge Room. A sergeant with a bald freckled head stood behind a flat desk. There was a large ledger-type book open in front of him with an array of pens and an old-fashioned inkwell.

"Empty your pockets!" ordered Denton.

The pit of Jubal's stomach collapsed. "You're joking," he said feebly.

The three uniformed cops watched noncommittally as Denton came forward. "Empty your fucking pockets," he snarled. "And I mean *everything!*"

Jubal obeyed in a daze, going through the motions for the second time in twenty-four hours. He put keys, money, and lighter on the desk, the almost-empty cheroot package. His mouth was very dry. He wanted to speak but the words wouldn't come.

Denton ran his hands lightly over Jubal's outer clothing and felt under his belt. Then he stepped behind Jubal, leaving the three uniformed men beyond the prisoner.

Jubal was suddenly conscious that fingers were exploring his hip pocket. He heard Denton's voice.

"And what about this? Or had you forgotten it?"

Jubal turned quickly. Denton was holding up a block of what appeared to be chewing tobacco wrapped in cellophane. Denton scraped off a fragment of the block and held it to his nose. He smiled at the desk sergeant, his eyes full of the strange brilliance.

"We've got a capture here, sergeant. A real capture. There must be half a pound of the stuff."

The desk sergeant peered down at the wrapped block. "That'd be worth a lot of money, that would."

Jubal looked at their faces, hopelessly. Denton must have picked up the hash at the Yard. None of them had seen him plant the stuff. Jubal made a sudden dash for the exit. The younger cop brought him down with a flying tackle, twenty yards across the cobblestones. They frogmarched him back to the station and charged him. Denton signed the sheet.

"Watch him, sergeant," he warned. "He's a long-distance runner."

The sergeant dropped the block of hash into a canvas sack. "Not in here, he isn't. Take his shoes and belt away and lock him up."

Jubal shuffled down the corridor in his socks, holding his trousers up with one hand. He could no longer trust himself to speak. The cop opened a cell. Inside was a plank bed with one thin blanket and a lavatory bowl at the far end. The walls were tiled and a patch of the summer evening showed beyond the high barred windows.

"In you go!" The cop was friendly enough.

Jubal found his voice. "I want to make a phone call."

The cop nodded amiably. "Who doesn't!" The door was slammed shut.

12. John Raven

THEY LAY side by side on the bed in the darkness, lulled by the houseboat's gentle rocking. It was some time since either had spoken. A shaft of light from the sitting room colored Kirstie's naked body amber. She rolled away from him and turned the face of the clock on the table. Then her fingers found his.

"It's twenty minutes to ten. You promised."

"I know," he said. She was off by five minutes but it didn't matter. There'd been no sign of Jubal, no word. Waiting any longer was useless. He reached for the phone and dialed Jerry Soo's number.

"It's me," he said. "Is it OK if Kirstie and I come over? I mean right now."

"Of course it's all right!" Soo sounded surprised. "Where are you speaking from?"

"We're on the boat. There's a whole lot of trouble and I need your advice."

A mosquito whined in the half-light. Kirstie slapped at it. "What sort of trouble?" asked Soo.

"You name it, we've got it," Raven told him. "Someone set the boat alight for starters. Then I got hold of Jubal. He and Denton framed Jamie all right but Jamie wasn't innocent."

He heard Soo sigh exasperatedly. "What is that supposed to mean?"

"He wasn't telling the truth in court. The real story is

that he'd been dabbling in stolen property for some time. That's why it was so easy to set him up. I took Jubal to Macfarlane's lawyer. He made a statement admitting everything but he didn't sign it. Now I've lost him."

Kirstie had left the bed for the bathroom. He could see her elongated shadow through the half-open door. "Jerry?" he asked quickly. There had been no sound for fifteen or twenty seconds.

"I'm here," said Soo. "You lost him."

"That's right," Raven said patiently. "I'll explain when I see you. The thing is that Jubal and Denton are out there somewhere, either together or apart, and Denton knows that *I* know."

Soo's voice took on sudden purpose. "You'd better get over here right away. And bring Kirstie with you."

Raven swung his long shanks off the bed. "OK," he called. "Get your clothes on. We're going over to Jerry's."

They dressed rapidly and Raven locked up. Saul Belasus was playing Duke Ellington. Raven had the same record, *Back to Back*. They crossed the plank. Saul's wheelhouse door was ajar and swinging. The smell of a joint drifted out. Raven and Kirstie stood at the top of the steps, waiting for a lull in the traffic to run for the far side. She touched his sleeve.

"I'm sure we're doing the right thing, darling."

Right thing, wrong thing. They were doing what circumstance had forced upon them. He smiled to himself. This was what it was all about, supposedly. Compromise. But not too damn much of it. The traffic thinned and they ran, hand in hand. The alleyway where he parked was dark, the bulb having seemingly failed. They walked up toward the Citroën. Raven put his key in the door as Denton emerged from the deep shadow behind the car. He was carrying an automatic in his left hand. His right hand collected Kirstie and pulled her close.

"*Now!*" he said, over her shoulder. "No wrong moves if you want her to stay alive." He gestured with the barrel of the gun, bringing Raven round to his side of the car. Denton glanced right and left along the Embankment. "After this next truck. *Right!*"

They halted at the top of the steps, Denton staring down at the burned wreckage that had been Raven's gangway. His eyes lingered on the plank leading from Saul's boat. The music was still playing below, the door still swinging, but there was no sign of the Californian. Denton jerked his head for Raven to lead the way down. Kirstie came next with Denton close behind. They negotiated the plank and made their way to the port side of the boat. Raven unlocked the sitting-room door and waited for further instructions.

"Curtains," snapped Denton. Raven touched the button and the curtains ran. "Lights," said Denton. He locked and bolted the door behind them. He grabbed Kirstie's arm and pulled her with him, peering briefly into the kitchen. Raven heard them go from one bedroom to the other. Then Denton reappeared, holding one of the two pairs of handcuffs. He was chuckling as he fastened Raven's left wrist to Kirstie's right and sat them on the sofa.

Denton's eyes were bright and confident. He looked from Raven to Kirstie, challenging them both. "Where's the tape?"

Raven shook his head. Denial was useless since Jubal would have talked. The only thing to do was stall for time.

"It's not here," he said.

Denton's smile slid away craftily. "I had a feeling you'd say that." He walked deliberately to the desk, opened drawers at random, and threw the contents on the floor. The smile was replaced with dark anger directed at Raven. Denton was breathing heavily.

"You meddlesome bastard! Why are you trying to ruin my career?"

Raven raised his shoulders. "You're doing that yourself."

It was the wrong thing to say and Denton's face reddened. He bent lower so that his eyes were on the same level as Raven's.

"I know all about you, Raven. You're sick, a frustrated ex-cop. But this is one that you lose, my friend. And you'd better understand that I do mean business."

"The tape's not here," Raven said steadily.

Denton's attention switched to Kirstie. "And there's something that *you'd* better understand! Your brother was a thief, a villain. I put him where he belonged."

Kirstie's green eyes widened. But her chin came up and she showed no sign of fear. Denton nodded to himself with mock surprise.

"I don't impress you too much, is that it?" He leaned forward and placed the barrel of the automatic in the middle of her forehead. "I'm going to count to ten. If no one's told me where the tape is by then, I'm pulling the trigger." He started to count.

Raven felt Kirstie's body shaking. "She doesn't know!" he burst out desperately. "I took it to Lassiter."

Denton stopped counting. "When?"

"When Jubal didn't come back to the car. That's where I went."

Denton shifted the gum he was chewing, scanning Raven's face. He made his decision. He found Lassiter's listings in the telephone directory, and put the book in Raven's lap, open. There were two entries. Office and home.

"Call him!" ordered Denton. "Tell him you must have the tape tonight. You'll go and collect it."

Raven pulled the small table toward him, the phone book still in his lap. Sweat was dripping, ice-cold, on his flanks. He glanced down at the book, affecting to read as he dialed Soo's number. He could feel his heart thudding in his rib-cage. A click sounded as the phone was lifted at the other end. Denton was watching narrowly.

"Mr. Lassiter? It's John Raven. Look, I'm in trouble over that tape I left with you this afternoon. I have to have it back. No, the morning won't do. I have to have it now." The line was open but Soo had not uttered a word. Raven continued. "You will? That's great. Thanks a lot, Mr. Lassiter. I'll be over."

He replaced the phone and dabbed at his forehead nervously. The salt sweat still managed to get beneath the strip of tape on his eyebrow.

"He's got tne tape at home. He'll give it to me."

Denton unlocked the cuff on Raven's left wrist and fastened Kirstie's two hands together. He raised the barrel of the automatic significantly.

"There's one in the breech and seven in the clip. It's twenty minutes past ten. Forty minutes to get to Cheam, five there and forty back. If you're not here by midnight, *with the tape*, your girlfriend's had it. Believe me, Raven. Everything I've worked for is at stake and it's neck or nothing."

Raven nodded, rubbing his chafed wrist. "I'll be back."

Denton undid the door leading out on deck. The music was still playing on the neighboring boat, the river peaceful under the moon.

"Midnight," said Denton. "And no tricks. I'm a better cop than you ever were and I know the game. I want no phone calls, no excuses. Just the tape. If you do this right, you've both got a chance."

Raven ran, checking his pockets as he skidded across the plank. Keys and money. It was odd that Denton hadn't searched him but then the cop was acting strangely. "Neck or nothing," he'd said, and maybe that was the clue. Raven flew up the steps and sprinted for the alleyway. The nearest phones were on Manresa Road. The first booth he tried had been vandalized. The second held the stale reek of urine but the phone worked.

Louise sounded scared, her voice like a ten-year-old's. "Jerry's gone to the Yard. He wants you to meet him there. You're to ask for Commander Grace's office. Is Kirstie all right, John?"

"I can't talk," he said. "No time." He put the phone down and ran back to the car. His thoughts had gone no further than Jerry. Wise, mocking, and completely reliable. Someone who hadn't failed him in seventeen years.

Raven slammed the Citroën into the curb, turned off the motor, and hurried into the concrete-and-glass building. A few people with the appearance of being troubled in spirit huddled on the benches. Raven made for the desk.

"Commander Grace's office, please. My name is Raven."

The girl was young with the clean asexual look of the uniformed policewoman. She used the telephone and nodded.

"Someone's coming down."

"I know my way up," he said. "And I'm in a hurry."

She turned cold blue eyes on him. "I'm afraid civilians aren't allowed on the upper floors without an escort. Security."

He was halfway across the hallway when he heard his name called. Soo was coming from the elevators, dressed in a poplin Windbreaker, slacks, and basketball shoes, as though he'd pulled on the first things that came to hand. He wasted no time, turning on his heel as Raven neared. The elevator started its upward journey. The Hong Kong-born cop's eyes sought Raven's face.

"Kirstie?"

Raven glanced down. He hadn't noticed before that his hands were shaking. "Bad. Denton's got her on the boat. He jumped us with a gun in the alleyway."

The elevator stopped. Soo put his hand on Raven's arm, detaining him in the corridor. "Is there anything I need to know before we see Grace? I've given him an idea of things."

Raven shook his arm free. "There's no time to tell it all twice, Jerry. Let's get going. We've only got until midnight."

They walked along the corridor, Soo talking as they went. He had put two and two together after Raven's phone call and suspected what might have happened. He had come straight to the Yard. Philip Grace was the Duty Commander.

"Jesus *Christ*, Jerry!" Raven said desperately. "Denton's a killer. I know it. We've got to get Kirstie out of there."

"Easy," said Soo, stopping. He knocked on a door and turned the handle. The large room was well-carpeted and furnished in the style supplied to the higher ranks at New Scotland Yard. A massive desk, open-fronted bookcase, and cloth-upholstered chairs. The man behind the desk was in his late fifties with short sandy hair and the broken-veined complexion of one who has spent much of his life in the open air. He was wearing a gray flannel suit with a rosebud in the buttonhole. The man standing in front of the window was younger. Raven vaguely remembered his face.

"Commander Grace and Chief Superintendent Pollock," said Soo. "This is Mr. Raven, sir."

Raven placed Pollock as a firearms specialist with a decoration for bravery. "Sit down, Mr. Raven," Grace invited.

"I'd sooner stand," said Raven. Grace waved a hand.

There was a picture of a teen-aged girl on a pony in front of him. "Inspector Soo's already told me something of your story. I'd like to hear the full details."

Raven talked for ten minutes. Grace made notes but no one interrupted. "There's no time to waste," Raven finished. "A woman's life is at stake."

Grace put his pen down. "It might interest you to know that I've been looking at your service record."

"It doesn't interest me at all," replied Raven.

Grace's lower teeth were crowded, giving him the look of a bulldog when he smiled.

"You seem to make a career of doing the work of A six, exposing dishonest policemen. You're making serious allegations against an officer with an impeccable record."

It was hot in the room and Raven was sweating. "I don't like your tone," he said. "I'm a civilian. Your officer with an impeccable record is standing with a gun at a woman's head at this very moment and I want something done about it. *Now!*"

Soo caught Raven's eye but too late. "Where *is* the tape?" Grace asked mildly. He seemed to have taken no offense.

"On my neighbor's boat," said Raven.

"And what do you expect Denton to do if you give it to him?"

"I expect him to kill us both," answered Raven. The thought had been in his head for some time but it sounded no worse said out loud.

Grace unfolded a linen-backed ordnance map. It was large-scale and covered the London stretch of the Thames.

"Show me exactly where your boat is."

The four men gathered around the desk as Raven located the *Albatross*. "The entrance door from the deck is on the river side. If the curtains are drawn, there's no way at all of seeing what's going on inside."

Grace glanced up over his shoulder at Pollock. "What about the river police?"

Pollock moved his head from side to side. "I think the roofs are a better idea, sir. I know the houses in that part of the world. We could cover this boat with cross-fire."

Raven stared at Soo. "What's going on here, Jerry?" He turned to Commander Grace. "What the hell are you talking about, people on roofs with guns, river police. Don't you understand? This girl's living on borrowed time. Denton's a cop. He knows what the score is. He'll be looking out for just that sort of thing and the moment he realizes what's happening, he'll blow her head off."

Grace's tone stiffened. "I agreed to see you because of what Inspector Soo told me. But I'll confess I'm at a loss. What did you come here for?"

"I came for help," said Raven. "Help to do things my way."

"And what is your way?" From stiffness Grace had come to sarcasm.

Raven licked his lips and aimed his words at his friend. "I'm getting out of here, Jerry."

Soo restrained him. "Take it easy, John. We're all trying to help."

Grace was on his feet, speaking with quick decision. "I'm taking charge of this myself. I want six marksmen and no more than two cars on the double. We've got to move fast."

Pollock was already on his way to the door. Grace locked his drawer and put the key in his trouser pocket. He came around the desk to Raven.

"Nothing will be done behind your back. You have my word on it."

Grace cut all the lights in the room save one and took a dark felt hat from a hook behind the door. This he placed squarely on his head and sniffed at his rosebud.

"I'll see you downstairs," he said, and vanished through a door further along the corridor.

Raven looked after him skeptically. "Do you suppose that he means me, as well?"

"Why don't you come off it, John!" Soo's normally equable face was exasperated. "Stop being so spiky. It's not going to help anything. Grace is a good man. Slow, maybe, but thorough."

Raven matched his friend's shorter stride along the corridor. Jerry must have sweated blood to set this interview up, even as a popular officer with a reputation for reliability. The story, such as he had known it up to an hour or so ago, must have sounded questionable, to say the least. Nor could the mention of John Raven's name have helped. Yet Jerry had somehow managed to impress Grace sufficiently for the man to listen and act.

"I'm sorry," Raven said impulsively.

Soo's smile came and went. "Never apologize."

There was a lighted clock above the elevators. Black hands said four minutes past eleven. The cage dropped like a stone, leaving part of Raven's stomach on the seventh floor. A ring of marksmen in plain clothes stood at the far end of the hallway, being briefed by Chief Superintendent Pollock. Grace had not yet appeared. They could have been part of any crowd but Raven knew that their jackets covered weapons and bulletproof vests. One of them was carrying a high-powered lantern and a loudspeaker. They were going in like a cavalry charge, he thought with despair.

"Let's get out of here," he said suddenly.

The short, squat Chinese in his pale blue Windbreaker and basketball shoes was a welcome relief after the derring-do at the other end of the hallway. Jerry was the only help he needed and Jerry was there. Police cars were ghosting to the entrance as the two men crossed the street to the Citroën. Raven moved the car off fast. As he turned right onto Victoria Street, he thought he heard the sound of a police siren. Once in Chelsea, he drove west on King's Road. A side street allowed him to approach the Embankment close to the Herborium. He reversed into the darkened alleyway and cut the motor. The houseboats floated twenty feet below the stone parapet opposite. It was impossible to see them or be seen from them. He turned his wrist. Eleven twenty-five. He opened the door on his side.

"You wait here," he instructed and went to the mouth of the alleyway. Blobs of brightness traced the outlines of the bridges. The traffic along the Embankment had thinned to the occasional rumble and flash of headlights. The pink glow from the power station illuminated the sky above the south bank of the river. There were no pedestrians. He crossed the road and looked down over the wall. A light showed in the wheelhouse of Saul's boat but the *Albatross* was in darkness. There was no sign of movement aboard, nothing but the gentle rise and fall of the deck. Suddenly police cars appeared from both directions. They slowed a couple of hundred yards away from the boats then swung across the road, blocking both east- and west-bound traffic. Raven sprinted for the alleyway. Soo was standing in the Herborium doorway.

Raven's voice was outraged. "What the hell do they think they're doing?"

Soo moved his stocky shoulders. Figures from the police cars were merging into the shadows and doorways of the houses on the north side of the Embankment. The pub was closed but the bars were still lit. Raven recognized Commander Grace's silhouette by his hat.

"What the hell are they doing, Jerry?" Raven repeated.

Soo looked up. "You know damn well what they're doing. Pollock's putting his men in place."

"You've got to stop it." Raven's voice was loud in the doorway. "Hold them up!"

"I know how you feel," Soo said quietly. "But how can I *do* that? I'm not sure that I'm even supposed to be here."

Raven shoved him farther back in the doorway. "You listen to me, Jerry. Kirstie's down there with a gun at her head. Those clowns are making sure that the trigger is pulled." He felt his hand being gently removed from Soo's chest.

"They're pros, John," said Soo. "And Grace is no fool. He's not going to put Kirstie's life at risk."

"What the fuck are you talking about," said Raven. "Her life *is* at risk!"

He stared down at his friend. People were supposed to pray in moments like this but midnight mass on Christmas Eve was the closest he had come to God in twenty years. He swallowed the lump in his throat. He could feel the tension between them.

"I'm going, Jerry," he warned. "Don't try to stop me."

"Going where?" Soo's voice was completely under control.

Raven jerked his head at the river. The Embankment was strangely still. The lights in the pub had gone out. People were still up in some of the houses, unaware of what was happening on the street below. Soo's head slanted.

"Go ahead. I'm not stopping you."

"Get hold of Grace," said Raven. "I'm going down on the boat. This is going to work, Jerry, one way or another. What time do you have?"

Soo looked at his gun-metal Ingersoll. "Twenty-two minutes to midnight."

Raven checked with his own watch. "Denton's going to keep his word. If I'm not on deck by five to twelve, hit him with everything. OK?"

"OK," Soo said quietly.

They touched hands and Raven ran across the deserted Embankment. There were no shouts, no signals, no attempt to stop him, though the marksmen and Grace must have seen him go. A streetlamp lighted the stone steps leading down to Saul's boat. Raven counted them as if the number were important. There were twenty-two, cut in the face of the granite retaining wall. The last few were slippery from the rise and fall of the river. He'd be exposed all the way down, like a fly on a piece of white paper. His plan grew more hazardous as the seconds ticked away but there was no going back. He could see now that the drapes were closed in his sitting room, kitchen, and both bedrooms. This could be in his favor unless Denton was in there with his eye to a chink in the curtains. Raven took a deep breath and held it till he reached the bottom of the steps. He hurled himself over the low railings onto the deck and went down on his stomach. The wheelhouse door was open. It swung to and fro with the movement of the boat. Its slow rhythmic banging combined with the slap of the river and grinding of chains. The Great Dane appeared in the doorway, yawned massively, and retreated again. Raven wriggled forward over the bilge-stop at the bottom of the door. The wheelhouse was empty. There was a dirty coffee cup on the folding card table and the tin ashtray was full of roaches. The air was acrid with the stink of cannabis.

Raven raised himself cautiously, keeping his head well below the wheelhouse windows. A light was on at the bottom of the companionway. Saul Belasus was sitting bolt upright in a chair by his bunk, the Great Dane beside him, its tail sweeping the floor as it looked up at Raven. Raven climbed down into the cabin, shaking his head despairingly as he saw the mindless smile on the Californian's face. The cabin was in disorder, the row of clothing swinging on the line. Raven grabbed Saul by the shirt with two hands and shook him. Mint candies scattered over the floor. Saul's head rolled loosely. Raven ran to the shower stall, filled an enamel jug with cold water, and tipped it over Belasus. The Californian sat quite still for a couple of seconds, then broke out of his shock, spluttering. Raven shook him again.

"Can you understand what I'm saying?"

Water was dripping from Saul's head and beard. His T-shirt and jeans were soaking. His eyes were trying to focus behind his steel-rimmed spectacles.

"I'm with you, man," he mumbled, still smiling benignly.

"Jesus *Christ!*" Raven said hopelessly. The Californian was in another world. There was no time to waste on coffee. He had to get through to him somehow and *now*. He took Saul's face in his hands and forced the bearded chin up. *"Kirstie,* Saul! Do you remember Kirstie?"

Belasus moved his head. "Then listen," said Raven. "She's on my boat with a bastard who's going to blow a hole in her head unless we stop him. You've got to help me, Saul."

Belasus freed himself from Raven's grasp and attempted to stand but fell back. He made it the second time by hanging onto the Great Dane's collar. He was rocking on his feet but seemed to have more control over his speech.

"Help," he said. "Sure."

Raven reached down into the dog's bed and came up with the tape-recorder. He held it in front of Saul's face.

"See this? It's what this guy's after. Do you think you're capable of taking his mind off Kirstie for a couple of minutes? That's all I need, a couple of minutes."

Belasus propped himself against the companionway, staring down at his drenched clothing as though he had only just noticed its condition.

"I'm relying on you," urged Raven. "Do you think you can do it?"

Belasus nodded. "I'm getting there, John. Don't worry, I'm putting it together." He giggled self-consciously.

Raven held the tape-recorder up again. "I want you to take this across to my boat. Hold it up in the air and shout to be sure that he sees you coming."

Belasus lurched sideways. "Hey, man. That's great."

Raven plucked the Californian's spectacles from his nose and slapped his face hard. The Great Dane rumbled warningly. Raven replaced the spectacles.

"Concentrate!" Raven pleaded. "Get a hold on yourself. This man is desperate. He'll do exactly as he says. Kirstie's dead unless we can fool him."

Belasus straightened the spectacles on his nose and took the tape-recorder from Raven. The Californian's jeans were still dripping water but his enunciation was clear and deliberate.

"Bet on me, John. You can bet on me."

Raven took a good look at him and gambled. Raven was first up the companionway. He cut the lights in the wheelhouse, gave Belasus a hand, and closed the door firmly on the dog. The scene outside hadn't changed. The sound of a radio or record player floated from one of the neighboring boats. The top stories of the houses facing the river soared unassailable and harmless, high above the stone retaining wall and parapet. The *Albatross* was still in total darkness. Raven took the knife Belasus had used for shaving his hash. He pulled the Californian close and breathed in his ear.

"We've got to have split-second timing on this or I'm dead too. I'm going to cut one of your ropes and go over the side. The moment you see me start to swing, you shout. OK? Pay no attention to anything else but keep walking. You hold the tape-recorder above your head so that he can see it."

The wheelhouse door continued to bang. Moonlight

silvered the rippling water. Belasus was pumping determination into each word and movement. Raven was conscious of the effort.

Saul cleared his throat softly. "Do I give this guy the tape-recorder?"

"It won't come to that," said Raven, and hoped that he was right. "The thing is to make sure that he sees you. I'll do the rest." He held his watch to the crack in the companionway door. It was fourteen minutes to midnight. He straightened up. "Jump in the river if the worst comes to the worst," he said, and dropped on his stomach again. He wriggled out of the wheelhouse to the low rails. Saul's boat was chain-moored like most of the others but a half-inch nylon rope ensured that her bows faced upstream. The unused length was coiled around a stanchion. He sawed through the rope and heard the severed end hit the water below. He uncoiled the twenty-odd feet that were left and snaked across the deck to the port side. He knotted one end of the rope to a matching stanchion. Holding the nylon line, he eased his body through the railings and lowered himself hand-over-hand. There was no sign of Saul.

Raven hung there, legs dangling above the river. No more than six feet separated the two boats but he was almost that distance below the deck of the *Albatross*. He had to swing to gain impetus, scrabbling with his sneakers and letting himself go, hoping to grab something that would give him a handhold. There were only two possibilities. A mooring-chain fastened to the bow of the *Albatross* and her bulwark. The bulwark was almost a foot across. The chain seemed safer. He propelled himself forward and kicked. The boat rolled slightly as he swung, scraping his shoulder along the side.

A shout split the peace of the reach. Saul had taken him literally. Raven swung again, letting himself go like a trapeze artist in free flight. His chest hit the chain hard and he clung to it, his fingers aware of the grinding links. He chinned himself painfully, making the last few inches with his eyes closed and his veins bursting. He rolled over, his stomach resting on the heavy chain. Then he eased himself sideways and dropped onto his own deck.

He stayed as he landed, crouched in the bow, almost under his bedroom windows. Belasus was halfway across the connecting planking, holding the small tape-recorder high in his hand and teetering dangerously. His spectacles glinted in the moonlight. His voice cracked as he shouted again, the echo chasing itself across the river to die on the other side. The tub with the rose bush in it where Raven had hidden his gun was twelve feet away, between him and the door from the deck to the sitting room. He started crawling forward then froze. The sitting-room door was being opened with infinite care, the handle firmly gripped, the weight of the door lifted so that the hinges wouldn't betray the leaver. Denton's head appeared. The Californian was somewhere on the other side of the superstructure now, near the burned-out gangway. Denton emerged from the doorway cautiously. His back was to Raven and he was holding his gun in his left hand. He was looking toward the stern of the houseboat. Raven tensed to jump him. There was no time to retrieve his own weapon. But Denton moved away, his back flat against the sitting-room windows, left hand extending his gun. And then he was out of sight.

A single shot whined across the water. A flash from a window high above the Embankment located the marksman. Raven hurled himself back instinctively, into the shelter of the bow. He heard the splash as Belasus took him at his word and went over the side. The next Raven heard was Kirstie's voice and Denton's angry reply. A steady thrash of arms through water indicated the Californian's progress. He was swimming for the south bank. Raven was on his feet again, standing as Denton had done with his back against the cedar planks. The shot had brought people up from their beds on the neighboring boats, some in pajamas, a couple with a crying baby, two people Raven had never seen before. They were all looking shoreward. A bright beam of light probed the *Albatross* as far as it could and settled on the stern.

Commander Grace's voice came bluff and challenging over the loud-speaker.

"This is Commander Grace, Denton. Give yourself up while you've got a chance!"

Something moved inside the sitting room. There was a scuffle then Kirstie's cry. They came out together, Denton's right arm locking Kirstie in front of him, his free hand presenting the gun at her head.

"I want you out of here!" called Denton. "Everyone except Grace. And I want him in a car at the top of the steps with the motor running."

Midnight chimed from a nearby church, disturbing the sudden silence. Lights had come on in windows along the Embankment.

Grace was back on the loud-speaker. "Let the girl go! I'll take her place!"

"No way!" yelled Denton. "I'm taking you both!"

Raven's finger dug deep in dirt as he felt for the plastic bag. He pulled the gun out and crept past the sitting-room windows. The Great Dane was barking. Raven's back was cold with sweat. He had to do this right. There'd be no second chance. His sneakers made no noise as he turned the corner into the powerful beam of light. Denton was facing the shore, his body protected by Kirstie's. The tape-recorder lay on the deck where Saul had dropped or

thrown it. Four more paces would take Raven within striking distance. Denton's back was to him but they could
certainly see him from the shore.

Denton's voice echoed across the water. "I'm going to
start walking now. If you're not in the car, Grace, by the
time I get to the top of the steps, she's had it, remember.
I've got nothing to lose."

There was a flash of yellow dress as Denton pushed
Kirstie sideways, still using her as a shield. He must have
hurt her. Raven leaped forward, hearing her yelp of pain.
He smashed the butt of the thirty-eight hard at the back of
Denton's skull. He saw the skin split and blood spurt. Den-
ton fell like a stunned steer, going down on his knees and
pitching forward. Kirstie bent down and snatched up
Denton's gun. Her feet were bare and her makeup had
run, leaving black tear streaks. Then suddenly she was in
Raven's arms.

He was conscious of movement above, more lights,
shouts, the wail of approaching police sirens. Commander
Grace and Soo were first on deck, Grace out of breath. The
plainclothesmen who followed rolled Denton over on his
back. His eyes opened and he spat as he looked up at
Raven. The detectives hauled him upright and led him
away, blood streaming through the fingers on his head.
Grace took the gun gently from Kirstie. Jerry Soo picked
up the tape-recorder. A uniformed cop was hanging over
the parapet, looking down at the people on the neighboring boats.

"The show's over. You can go back to bed!"

"Are you all right, Miss Macfarlane?" The Commander's
voice was concerned.

"Thank you," she whispered, but Raven could feel her
shaking. They all went up to the street. Blinking amber
lights showed where the traffic had been diverted. There

was a brief glimpse of Denton in the back of a car that swept by with siren blaring. The tall elegant lamp-standards along the Embankment stood like sentinels guarding the peaceful river. Most of the lights in the windows had been extinguished again. Soo zipped up his poplin Windbreaker, his smile square as he offered the tape-recorder to Grace.

"I suppose you'd better take care of this, sir."

"Yes," Grace said absently. He was looking at Raven. "Have you any idea what you two have let yourselves in for? The hours of statements and explanations. Jubal's in Cannon Row We heard just a few minutes ago. Denton's charged him with something or other, something to do with drugs. It won't hold, of course."

A police car drew up at the curb, its driver waiting discreetly out of earshot.

"These statements and explanations," said Raven. "Can they wait until the morning? It's been a long day for everyone.

"Of course," said Grace "And vou'd better get hold of that lawyer, what was his name?

"Lassiter," said Raven.

Kirstie's bare feet were standing on his sneakers. She was no longer speaking in a whisper. Her tone was fierce and defensive. "He doesn't *need* a lawyer. He's done nothing wrong."

"That's exactly why he needs a lawyer," Grace said dryly. "To make it all sound right. Good night anyway. You can give me a ring in the morning." He glanced at Soo. "Are you coming with me, Detective-Inspector?"

"Thank you, sir. My car's at the Yard." Soo turned to Raven. "If you want to spend the night with us . . ." Grace had the car door open and was inside, waiting. "It's the best place for you," urged Soo.

"The best place for him is with me," Kirstie said clearly.

"You heard," added Raven. "The best place for me is with her. Good night, Jerry, and give our love to Louise."

They waited till the taillights disappeared and then walked down the steps. A trail of water across the deck showed that Saul had somehow managed to get aboard without being seen. Kirstie's tear-streaked face was tired but happy. Raven bent his head and kissed her mouth, long and hard.